SAY YES, SAMANTHA

Barbara Cartland, the celebrated romantic novelist, historian, playwright, lecturer, political speaker and television personality, has now written nearly two hundred books. She has had a number of historical books published and several biographical ones, including a biography of her brother, Major Ronald Cartland, who was the first Member of Parliament to be killed in the war. The book has a preface by Sir Winston Churchill.

In private life, Barbara Cartland is a Dame of Grace of St John of Jerusalem, and one of the first women, after a thousand years, to be appointed to the Chapter General. Miss Cartland has fought for better conditions and salaries for midwives and nurses, and as President of the Hertfordshire Branch of the Royal College of Midwives, she has been invested with the first Badge of Office ever given in Great Britain, which was subscribed to by the midwives themselves. She has also championed the cause of old people and had the laws regarding gypsies altered. She founded the first Romany Gypsy Camp in the world which was christened 'Barbaraville' by the gypsies.

Barbara Cartland is deeply interested in vitamin therapy and is President of the National Association for Health.

BARBARA CARTLAND

SAY YES, SAMANTHA

A Pan Original

Pan Books London and Sydney

First published 1975 by Pan Books Ltd,
Cavaye Place, London SW10 9PG
2nd printing 1976
© Barbara Cartland 1975
ISBN 0 330 24536 8
Printed in Great Britain by
Cox & Wyman Ltd, London, Reading and Fakenham

1928
Reflection 1

Of course I am ready too soon, as I always am when I'm nervous. I wish I wasn't going to this dinner party, but once Giles told me we had both been invited I knew that this time I could not back out of it.

I'm afraid of going to the Meldriths again because they are friends of David . . . but David is in America!

There was a long report the other day in *The Daily Express* about the film they are making of his book, so one thing is certain: David won't be there.

I can't meet him yet . . . I can't. Even to think of it makes me feel . . . terrified.

Yet I want to see him! I want it so much that every nerve in my body screams for him! Oh David! . . . David! . . . David!

I mustn't work myself up! I've told myself over and over again to be calm.

I'm going to use my brain – the brain I have only just discovered – to work things out logically and sensibly. Then I shan't be upset when I see David again. I shall be just as he wants me to be.

The first step is to be poised and sophisticated.

That is what I tell myself I'll be, and yet at the moment I have that same old stupid sick feeling inside me, and I know that when we arrive at the Meldriths' house I shall feel as if I have fifty butterflies fluttering about in my tummy.

I suppose the time will come when I'll be able to think of David without this agonising ache! Without having to fight every moment against a wild desire to telephone him just to hear his voice.

Why is love such sheer undiluted hell . . .?

I'll look at myself in the mirror. They always say good clothes give a woman confidence in herself, and this dress I borrowed from Norman Hartnell is, I think, one of the loveliest he's ever designed.

Would David think I was beautiful in it?

Stop! Stop wondering what he would or would not think! Face the fact, Samantha, that you bore him!

At this moment he will be with someone else far prettier than you! Someone amusing, witty, gay, experienced, and very intelligent! . . . Yes, very experienced and very intelligent! And I have neither of those qualities!

Giles was terribly pleased at being invited to the dinner tonight because Lady Meldrith is giving the party for Prince Vezelode of Russia.

She had telephoned Giles and said to him:

"You *must* come, Mr. Bariatinsky, and bring with you that glorious red-haired model of yours – Samantha Clyde."

Giles loves being thought a Russian because actually he's English!

His grandmother was a Bariatinsky, but his father was called Travis, or Trevor; but when he decided to become a photographer he took his grandmother's name.

It was a sensible thing to do, because people in England are always much more impressed by anything foreigners do than by their own efforts – I can't think why.

He told me to borrow a sensational dress, so I went along to see Norman Hartnell at his Salon in Bruton Street and he was charming about it.

He has been designing only for a few years since he left Cambridge and yet all the most important and glorious young people now buy their gowns from him.

He is young, boyish and full of enthusiasm, and he said to me:

"You know, I always like you to wear my clothes, Samantha. You look so exotic in them."

That's a good description of my looks, but I only wish I felt exotic inside.

However I shouldn't complain. I should be grateful really, because if I hadn't got red hair and large green eyes, I should still be in Little Poolbrook organising the Church bazaars.

Perhaps I would be happier if I had stayed there and never come to London – and never met David!

Is it really better to have 'loved and lost'?

Sometimes I think love is all the tortures of the devil. Then I remember those moments of unbelievable ecstasy when David swept me up into the sky and I touched the stars . . .

Reflection 2

It's funny how unexpected things happen in life.

When I got up that Saturday morning, five months ago, I had no idea that it was to prove a milestone – or should I say a turning-point? – in my life.

It was just like any other morning.

I awoke to hear the birds singing in the garden and thought that it was still very early and there was no need for me to hurry.

I suppose it was because I was nervous of over-sleeping after Mummy died that I made myself wake up at about seven o'clock every morning so that I could get Daddy's breakfast.

Of course on Sunday I had to be earlier still because the first Communion Service was at eight o'clock, and he liked to be in the Church at least twenty minutes before the congregation, if there was any, arrived.

Anyway, that Saturday, after I was awake I suddenly remembered that it was the day of the Church bazaar, and there were a million extra things to do.

I jumped out of bed, washed rather quickly and started to dress.

I was not going to put on my best dress, which was rather a pretty green muslin I had made myself, until the last moment. So I just slipped into one of my old cottons which was too tight. But it wasn't likely anyone was going to see me.

I ran downstairs, started to prepare breakfast, and found, when Daddy joined me, that he had forgotten all about the bazaar and thought it was just an ordinary Saturday.

He had got more and more forgetful after Mummy died, or perhaps his mind was so concentrated on remembering her and being so unhappy that it was difficult for him to think of anything else.

I gave him his breakfast, reminded him that he had promised to look in on the choir practice at nine-thirty, and told him to put on his best coat and a clean white collar before he came up to the Castle.

"Thank goodness it's a nice day," I said. "Otherwise, if it was like last year, we should be even more in debt than we are already."

"Yes, of course, Samantha, we should be grateful for the weather," Daddy said, rather in a tone of voice as if he was surprised he could be grateful for anything.

He had always been so happy and so gay when Mummy was there.

I felt sometimes like crying, knowing how difficult it was for him to make an effort to sound cheerful merely because he thought I expected it.

"Is Lady Butterworth opening the bazaar?" he asked.

8

"Of course she is, Daddy," I answered. "You know she wouldn't let anyone else have the honour and the glory."

I saw the expression on his face and knew that, if Daddy was capable of hating anyone, he hated Lady Butterworth.

Daddy was a Clyde, and the Clydes had owned the Castle since the Norman Conquest, or something like that. But they couldn't afford to keep it up, and it had got more and more dilapidated until the ceilings fell down and there were damp stains in every room.

Then the Butterworths had come along and bought it from Daddy's father – my grandfather – just before he had a stroke.

I don't think they paid very much for it. At the same time it had been a help, because when my grandfather died and his debts were paid the money was divided between Daddy and his sister.

The Butterworths then proceeded to 'do up' the Castle and live in it.

Sir Thomas Butterworth had made money in Birmingham, where he had enormous factories. Now because he was so rich, he and his wife wanted to be 'County'.

Of course, they hadn't the slightest idea how to set about it and the Castle, although luxurious, was furnished in excruciatingly bad taste.

I used to see Daddy wince as soon as he entered the Hall, and I always suspected that he shut his eyes in the Drawing-room.

But as I said to him once:

"Surely it is better for the Butterworths to live there than for it just to fall to the ground and become full of nothing but birds' nests and bats?"

For a moment I thought Daddy was going to storm at me and say that he hated the Butterworths spoiling everything with their money, and that he much preferred it as it was.

Then with what was an obvious effort he had said:

"They have been generous in the village, Samantha, and we must learn to thank God for small mercies."

Personally I find it difficult to think of Lady Butterworth, who must weigh at least fifteen stone, as being a 'small mercy', but in fact she has a kind heart.

She gave us heating in the Church which was something we never had before, a Pavilion for the cricket-field, and a water-trough on the green.

The last actually was quite unnecessary as there is a very good pond from which the horses still drink, ignoring the water-trough, but at least she 'showed willing'.

When I arrived at the Castle carrying baskets of cakes and garden produce for the Vicarage stall, Lady Butterworth was already re-organising everything and altering all the arrangements which had been familiar for years.

Mummy was the only person who never minded having to change the position of her stall or being told to re-arrange the cakes.

The other people in the village minded dreadfully.

I saw as soon as I got there that they were all muttering beneath their breath and looking resentful.

Knowing it was my job, I tried to pour oil on troubled waters.

"You are late, Samantha," Lady Butterworth said, severely.

"I'm sorry," I answered, "but I had a lot of things to do before I could get here."

"I can think of nothing that is more important than our own special Church bazaar," Lady Butterworth said, with a beaming smile.

I nearly replied that as the Castle was packed with servants she had nothing else to do!

There was no doubt that she enjoyed every moment of the bazaars, village concerts, and even the Church meetings at which she talked far more than anyone else.

In my opinion she found it lonely at the Castle after living in Birmingham.

I expect she had friends there who popped in to see her, whilst at the Castle she sat alone in her glory, hoping against hope that one of 'the County' would call on her.

"Poor thing," Mummy said once. "I am sorry for her. She is like a fish out of water. You know as well as I do, Samantha, that even if the Hudsons, the Burlingtons and the Croomes accepted the Butterworths, they would have nothing in common."

I think it was pity which made Mummy go out of her way to be kinder and in a way more effusive to Sir Thomas and Lady Butterworth than she was to anyone else.

Mummy never worried about being social and like Daddy, she hated parties.

"I gave them all up when I married your father," she said to me once. "I was very gay when I was young, Samantha, and then I fell in love."

"Didn't you miss the Balls, doing the London Season, and being presented at Buckingham Palace?" I asked.

Mummy laughed.

"I can honestly say, Samantha, and you know I never lie, that I have never for one moment regretted marrying your father and being terribly poor, but very, very happy."

It was only after the War when I got older that Mummy began to wish sometimes that I could enjoy 'coming out' as she had.

"I would love to present you at Court, Samantha," she said once, "but we just cannot afford it. I suppose, if your grandparents had been alive, it would have been different."

Mummy had been an only child and her parents had died during the War.

Although she had not seen much of them after she

married Daddy, since they lived in the North, I know she missed them once they were dead.

I think everyone, when they are orphaned, feels as if a prop or support has been knocked from under them.

I know that when Mummy died I felt as if I was missing an arm or a leg; and when Daddy went ... but I mustn't think about that!

But to go back to the bazaar, it started like every other bazaar that I had ever attended; the same disputes, the same disagreeableness, the same frantic search for drawing-pins to hold up the muslin draperies in front of the stalls, the same arguments over prices.

Mrs. Blundell, the Baker's wife, took umbrage because the iced cake she had made was not, in her opinion, priced high enough.

She was only slightly mollified when she learnt that Lady Butterworth had asked particularly that the cake should be reserved for her.

I seemed to be running hither and thither and ordered about by everyone, before the stalls were finally ready and the cakes and lavender-bags, doilies, knitted scarves and the other articles we had all been making, were arranged and Daddy arrived with a bag of small change so that every stall-holder would have some cash to start with.

I slipped home just before luncheon to get some food ready for Daddy and to snatch a bite myself.

I hadn't got to change my dress because I had put on the green muslin before I went up to the Castle.

I couldn't have gone in the dress I wore for breakfast but I did go up to my Bed-room to tidy my hair and collect the hat which I had trimmed myself especially for the occasion.

It was really very pretty, decorated with water-lilies and some green muslin left over from my new dress.

I thought it was just as good as some of the creations I had seen at Cheltenham which were priced at fifteen shillings!

I looked at myself in the mirror and hoped that no-one would think I was too over-dressed for the Vicar's daughter.

I was well aware that many of the ladies disapproved of my looks. I had heard one of them only the week before, saying:

"She's such a nice girl. It's a pity she looks so theatrical."

I had gone home and looked at myself in the mirror.

"Do I really look theatrical?" I asked.

Of course, my hair is red. I can't help that, but it is not a violent, ugly red. It has a kind of gold undertone so that it is quite a soft colour, although it does shine rather brightly when it is first washed.

My eye-lashes are long and very dark – I can't think why – and my eyes sometimes look green and sometimes grey.

Mummy always said I must be careful of my skin and insisted on my wearing a hat even when I went out in the garden, so my skin is very white, with just a faint touch of colour on the cheeks.

Certainly my new hat gave me a rather 'dressed-up' appearance, but then everyone dressed up for the bazaar, which was the most important event of the year as far as the village was concerned.

I suppose in a way it was more of a fête than a bazaar because the Church Wardens arranged races for the children.

There was also 'bowling for a pig' given by our richest and most important farmer, a hoop-la, a coconut-shy and skittles lent to us by the landlord of 'The George and Dragon'.

When I had a pony, there used to be pony-rides for tuppence each, but Snowball had now grown old and there had been no money with which to buy me a bigger horse.

I looked at my new hat again and pushed the water-lilies,

which I had bought very cheaply in a sale, a little flatter against the crown.

I couldn't see anything wrong with it, but I knew only too well how critical and fault-finding the people in the village were, especially the Church Wardens' wives.

Feeling rather self-conscious I went back to the Castle and slipped behind the Vicarage stall to await the customers.

There were three other people to help me and although hardly anyone had as yet arrived they said to me reproachfully:

"Where have you been, Samantha? We missed you."

"I had things to do at the Vicarage," I answered.

I wasn't going to admit that I had to cook Daddy's lunch because Mrs. Harris, our daily help, wouldn't come in on Saturdays when she had her husband home.

"Well, you are here now," one of the ladies said, "and that's a good thing, because Lady Butterworth intends to make her speech at exactly two o'clock and, as she is bringing a party down from the Castle, she expects us all to gather round so as to look a crowd."

Lots of people, I knew, would turn up later in the afternoon, but not until they had washed up after lunch and put on their best clothes. So I could understand Lady Butterworth not wishing to address what looked like an empty garden.

"Has she got a big house-party?" I asked curiously.

It was unlike her to have many people staying at the Castle except at Christmas-time, when they entertained all their relations.

"So she said," was the reply, "and she appeared to be in rather a fluster about them. They must be important."

It sounded interesting. At the same time I had my doubts. I had never seen anyone of any importance staying at the Castle.

However it was really not for me to judge because the only time we saw the Castle guests was in Church on

Sunday, and then so far as I knew only half of them might have turned up.

At five minutes to two I saw Lady Butterworth with quite a number of other people coming out of the garden door of the Castle which led straight on to the lawn where the stalls had been arranged.

The Castle made a perfect background for the bazaar, its grey stones looking gaunt and very impressive.

Standing outside, one mercifully could not see the dreadful variegated carpets or the Genoese velvet curtains with over-ornate fringes.

The army of gardeners employed by the Butterworths had clipped the yew-hedges, and the lilac and syringa were great fragrant splotches of mauve and white. The almond trees planted by my grandmother were a poem of pink and white blossom.

As Lady Butterworth's party came towards us I heard a man's voice say in what seemed to me to be a rather affected tone:

"It's very English."

And someone else said teasingly:

"Don't tell me, Giles, you haven't brought your camera!"

"I shall go back and get it," the man answered.

By the time the party had reached the platform on to which Lady Butterworth was mounting with some difficulty, we were all clustered round rather like a flock of sheep looking goggle-eyed at the party from the Castle.

They were certainly a different collection from anything I had ever seen before.

The women were really pretty and beautifully dressed, and the men were much younger than one would have expected Sir Thomas and Lady Butterworth's friends to be.

The man called Giles had turned to go back to the Castle, but Lady Butterworth saw him and gave a cry.

"You can't go back now, Mr. Bariatinsky," she called, "at least not until I have made my speech!"

"Of course not," he replied, with a smile.

I looked at him with interest.

He was rather nice-looking; thin and elegant with dark brown hair pushed back from an oval forehead.

A camera had been mentioned and I thought that he did look rather artistic. I noticed that his fingers were long and that he wore a signet ring with a green stone on one.

There was plenty of time to stare at the party while Daddy introduced Lady Butterworth, thanked her for lending the Castle grounds and praised her generosity and kindness to the village.

Then Lady Butterworth, smiling at the nice things he had said, made an almost impassioned appeal for everyone to spend a lot of money because it was so important that the Church should not be in financial difficulties, and there was so much to do in the forthcoming year.

I had heard it all so often before, so I didn't listen. I just looked at the house-party and realised how amateurish the green muslin dress I had made myself looked beside the dresses the women were wearing.

And I saw at once that my hat was over-decorated and quite the wrong shape.

Most of the women wore tiny cloche hats that fitted tightly over their ears like helmets and showed only a few wisps of hair on their cheeks.

Their dresses, too, were much plainer and straighter than mine.

Waists had risen a little in the last year, but the hem-lines had obviously dropped. My dress was too short and too full.

'Everything about me is wrong,' I thought with a sigh, and I found myself wondering if I could slip behind some bushes and cut the water-lilies off my hat.

I was still thinking about my appearance when Lady Butterworth finished her speech which was, of course, the
signal for a round of applause.

Then she accepted a bouquet of flowers from a small child
who was most reluctant at the last moment to part with it,
and started a triumphal tour of the stalls accompanied by
Daddy, with the house-party trailing behind her.

She shook hands with all the stall-holders as if she hadn't
seen them only an hour beforehand when we were getting
everything ready, and spent a considerable amount of
money, making poor Daddy and her guests carry the
cushions, woollen jumpers and the vegetables from the
Castle grounds which she bought.

When she arrived at the stall where I was selling she
shook hands with the other helpers but merely smiled at
me.

"I know you have been a very busy girl all day, Samantha," she said condescendingly, "and now you must persuade me to buy some of these delicious cakes so that
perhaps this stall will make more than all the others."

"We've kept the iced cake for you, Lady Butterworth," I
said.

"It looks delicious. We really must have it for tea," she
replied. "Perhaps, Samantha, you would be kind enough to
take it up to the Castle for me?"

"Yes, of course," I answered.

Then she turned away to make a difficult decision as to
whether she should buy more lavender bags or a scarf which
had been distressingly badly knitted by one of the older in-
habitants of Little Poolbrook.

I was wondering whether to take the cake up to the Castle
right away or wait until it was nearly tea-time, when a voice
said:

"Did I hear Lady Butterworth call you Samantha? It's a
very unusual name."

I looked up in surprise and found the man they had called 'Giles' was speaking to me.

"Yes, that's my name," I answered, rather stupidly.

He stood looking at me in such a strange way that I felt embarrassed.

He didn't speak again and I couldn't think of anything to say.

Yet I felt somehow as if I were waiting for something to happen.

Then as Lady Butterworth paid for the cake and her other purchases she said almost sharply:

"I think, Samantha, you had better take the cake up at once, otherwise it will melt in the sun, and there are quite a lot of flies about."

"Yes, of course, Lady Butterworth," I answered.

I was glad of an excuse to escape because I felt shy under this strange man's scrutiny. So I picked up the cake and, walking behind the other stalls, made my way in the direction of the Castle.

It was only when I reached the edge of the lawn where the stalls ended that I realised I was not walking alone.

Giles had joined me.

"I've an awful feeling," he said with a smile, "that we are going to be forced to eat that nauseating-looking concoction whether we like it or not."

I gave a little laugh.

"Lady Butterworth is very fond of iced cake, so perhaps she won't need your assistance."

"I hope you're right," he said. "I detest sweet things."

"Perhaps that's why you are so thin," I answered without thinking.

I was then afraid he might think it impertinent of me to make such a personal remark.

He didn't answer and after a moment, because I felt I had perhaps been rude, I said nervously:

"Are you going to photograph the bazaar?"

"It would be a waste of film," he answered. "But I should like to photograph you!"

"Me?" I looked up at him in surprise.

By this time we had reached the door of the Castle and I stopped, wondering whether I should walk in as the door was open, and put the cake down on a table, or whether I should ring the bell.

Giles made the decision for me.

"Come along," he said. "We'll give that cake to one of the footmen, and then I want you to do something for me."

I was too surprised to argue. I just followed him along the passage which led to the main Hall.

It looked very different with its coloured-glass windows and a black and white checked marble floor, from its appearance in my grandfather's day.

There were two footmen in resplendent livery with silver buttons and striped waistcoats standing by the front door.

Giles called one of them over.

"Her Ladyship wants this cake for tea."

"Very good, Sir," one of the footmen answered respectfully.

He took the cake from me and then Giles said:

"Come this way."

He opened the door of the Drawing-room.

As usual I could not help wondering why Lady Butterworth had chosen to have so many colours clashing with each other until the room looked like one of those kaleidoscopes one buys at a penny-bazaar.

Giles walked into the middle of the room and stopped.

"Now," he said, "take off that elaborate confection you have on your head. I want to look at you."

I stared at him in astonishment.

"Do you mean my hat?"

"If that is what you call that period piece – I do," he answered. "Take it off!"

I was too surprised and too humiliated to argue. I merely did as he told me.

I took off my hat and stood in the sunshine coming through the long windows which led out on to the terrace.

"It's unbelievable!" he exclaimed.

"I trimmed it myself," I said apologetically, "but I see now it's not right."

"I'm not talking about your hat," he replied sharply, "but your hair."

"My hair?"

I looked at him wide-eyed.

"And your eye-lashes. Look down!"

I came to the conclusion that he was a lunatic. No-one else would behave in such a way!

But because he embarrassed me I looked away from him, first at the carpet and then sideways across the room, wondering if the best thing to do would be to escape from him through one of the open windows.

"Incredible!" he exclaimed. "Absolutely incredible! Now tell me who you are."

"My name is Samantha Clyde," I answered, "and my father is the Vicar of Little Poolbrook."

"Your background is from Jane Austen," he said, "but you are too beautiful for one of her heroines."

Once again I looked at him, quite certain by this time that he was deranged.

"You must know you are quite beautiful, Samantha," he said after a moment.

"No-one has ever said that . . . before," I answered.

"Are there no men in Little Poolbrook?"

"Not many," I replied. "Most of the young ones were killed in the War, so we have a large percentage of grandfathers."

"Then that will account for it," he said. "Well, Samantha, let me tell you something – your face is your fortune!"

I gave a little laugh.

"There aren't any fortunes in Little Poolbrook, except here in the Castle."

"I'm not talking about this benighted hole," he replied. "I'm taking you to London. I'm going to photograph you, Samantha. I'm going to make you famous – you will become one of the most fabulous and best known faces in England!"

"It's very kind of you to think of such things," I answered, "but really I must be getting back to the bazaar. Otherwise they will be wondering what has happened to me."

"Damn the bazaar!" he exclaimed. "You are going to stay here and I'm going to take some pictures of you now. I want to be quite certain that you come out right in black and white. It's always difficult with red-heads. Now, don't move. Promise me you'll stay where you are until I come back."

"I . . . I don't . . . know," I stammered. "I . . . I don't think . . . I can."

"You'll do as you're told," he said sharply. "I won't be a moment."

He walked quickly across the Drawing-room as he spoke, went out of the room and shut the door.

I stood staring after him.

"He's crazy!" I told myself.

At the same time there was a little excited feeling inside me because he had said I was beautiful.

I knew some people thought I was pretty and Mummy had often said to me:

"You are going to be very pretty, Samantha. I do wish Daddy and I could give a Ball for you and you could have a dress like the one I wore when I came out."

She sighed and added wistfully:

"It was white satin, trimmed with tulle and pink rose-buds, and I thought it was the most beautiful gown in the whole world."

But as there was not enough money for me to have more than one or two very ordinary garments every year, like a winter coat, there certainly wasn't enough for a Ball-gown, let alone a Ball, and so I had never even thought about it.

But now this strange man had said I was beautiful!

I really hadn't moved since he left the room. Then because I was so curious about myself I walked to where there was a long gold-framed mirror between the windows.

I stared at my reflection and realised that my hair was in fact a very unusual colour.

It was not fashionably bobbed. Although I had chopped off the sides, I still had a rolled up bun at the back which I had not dared cut myself.

It waved naturally and some of the curls which had got untidy under my hat turned up and looked like little tongues of fire.

As I stared at myself in the mirror I thought that I didn't look as young and unsophisticated as I felt.

Perhaps my looks had altered through the years until they illustrated my name.

Mummy told me that when she was expecting me she had longed for all the expensive things they could not afford.

"I wanted to eat caviare and quails," she had told me, "chocolate creams and truffles, and drink champagne."

She gave a little sigh.

"Of course I never told your father. He would have been upset. I suppose it was the reaction to having had to be so frugal and cheese-paring during the first year of my married life!"

She smiled so that I would not think she regretted having married Daddy, before she continued:

"My papa would not give me much money. He always thought it a mistake for a woman to have money, and anyway he had been disappointed by my not having married someone richer and of more importance."

She laughed.

"Your father and I had only two hundred pounds a year between us in those days, and as I was a very bad housekeeper, I could not make it go very far."

"But you were glad that you were having me, Mummy?" I asked.

"Of course I was, darling. I longed for a baby and I hoped that if it was a daughter she would be very beautiful."

Mummy put her arms round me.

"I was so tired of the plain, tiresome little girls that I taught in Sunday-School that I used to pretend to myself that my daughter would look like a Princess in a fairy-tale – and you did, Samantha!"

"I'm so glad," I cried.

"So I said to your father after you were born: 'Our daughter is going to have an exciting name, so that she will be different from other children'."

Mummy had paused and then she went on:

"Your father said rather hesitatingly: 'I thought we might call her Mary after my mother and Lucy after my sister'."

"I hate both those names," I exclaimed, "but you gave them to me."

"I know," Mummy answered, "because I loved your father and didn't want to disappoint him. You were christened Mary Lucy, but I added Samantha because it was the most thrilling and exciting name I had ever heard."

So except when I had to write my name on examination papers at school, I have always ignored the common-place 'Mary Lucy'.

I was still looking at myself in the mirror when the door opened and Giles came back.

He carried a camera in his hands and a tripod under his arm.

He set up his equipment, grumbling as he did so:

"I hate taking photographs except in my studio! I want lights and backgrounds. I can see you against shimmering silver with a crystal chandelier just showing above your head. I can see you lying on a tiger-skin! I want you posed against black satin cushions with white balloons floating in the background!"

"Do you sell your photographs?" I asked.

"Of course," he answered. "I have a permanent arrangement with *Vogue*, but all other magazines want a 'Giles Bariatinsky', and I can assure you they pay me handsomely."

He made me sit, stand and even lie down on the carpet.

That made me terribly embarrassed in case someone came into the Drawing-room. They would have wondered what on earth I was doing.

Giles just fired orders at me, and although I felt guilty not to be helping at the bazaar it was somehow impossible not to obey him.

Finally when he had taken what seemed to me to be a hundred different shots he said:

"When can you come to London?"

"Come to London?" I repeated stupidly.

"I'm engaging you as one of my models," he said. "You are just the type of girl I have been looking for. I already have a blonde and a brunette. Now I shall have you."

"It's impossible!" I answered. "I live here."

"Don't be a fool!" he said. "You can't stay in Little Puddleduck, or whatever it's called, for the rest of your life!"

I laughed because he said it in such a funny way, but I replied quite seriously:

"I look after my father. He would not hear of my going to London."

24

"I'll have a talk with him," Giles said. "Come on."

He picked up his camera and tripod and I followed him.

I was to learn that when Giles said 'Come on' in just that tone of voice, one did exactly that.

I picked up my hat.

"There's no point in wasting time," Giles turned to say. Then he added: "For God's sake, go home and burn that monstrosity. It makes me sick just to look at it!"

Reflection 3

When I look at myself now, it is difficult to visualise what I must have looked like the first time Giles saw me.

Hartnell's dress has a skirt of topaz-coloured tulle on which are sewn tiger-lilies, with their petals and stamens glittering.

It is cut very low at the back, right down to the waist, with the bodice embroidered in topaz and gold beads which match my hair.

All the evening dresses are so pretty this Autumn. They fall to the ground at the back and lift a little at the front just to reveal my ankles and the topaz satin slippers which I wear over such transparently thin stockings that I feel they are almost indecent.

Giles had my hair bobbed when I first came to London, but now it is parted low on the left-hand side and sweeps across the front of my head in a huge wave to curl up at the back.

It is very alluring – at least that is what the gossip-writers say! All their descriptions of me begin:

"The alluring Samantha Clyde"

and

"The enigmatic Samantha Clyde."

Sometimes they are more romantic. I liked the one which began:

"Samantha Clyde smouldering with fire, mysterious as mountain mist."

I've learnt that the sideways glance which I inadvertently gave Giles the first time is what they call my 'enigmatic' look, and when my eyelids are slightly lowered I am described as 'exotic'.

Actually I half-shut my eyes because I'm shy, but of course the Press don't know that, and they think I personify the calculated allure of worldly sophistication, which, unfortunately, is very different from the truth.

I hope Giles will be pleased with my looks to-night.

Sometimes he is very disagreeable when he thinks I'm wearing a dress that doesn't suit me. But Hartnell was quite sure that 'Tiger-Lily', as this dress is called, was exactly the right gown for me and in fact I wore it in his Show.

One day I shall write a book and it will be all about my life and the strange things that have happened to me, and I shall call it, *Say Yes, Samantha*, because that is what people are always saying to me.

The first person to say it to me was Giles when we were walking back from the Castle to the bazaar and he said:

"I'm going to tell your father that you must come to London with me. You want to come, don't you?"

I didn't answer and he said insistently:

"You've got to come! You can't stay for ever in this God-forsaken place! So say yes, Samantha, and let's get on with it."

I really didn't get much chance of saying yes, or no.

We reached the bazaar to find that Daddy had gone home with the first 'takings' of the afternoon.

"He'll be coming back later," one of the helpers told me, but Giles would not wait.

"Show me the way to the Vicarage," he said, so we set off walking through the village and across the green.

"Why are you staying at the Castle?" I asked curiously. Then thinking it sounded rude, I added quickly:

"Lady Butterworth's friends are usually much older."

"There's a big Charity Ball being given in Cheltenham to-night," Giles answered. "The Countess of Croome, who is the Chairman, has asked everyone living round about to put up her friends from London."

That accounted, I knew, for Lady Butterworth being in a flutter about her party. She had been longing to get to know the Croomes.

I wondered if they would bother with her after her usefulness was over!

The Vicarage was next to the ugly Victorian Church which had been erected after the original Norman building had crumbled into dust.

I had always disliked its ugly interior, just as I have instinctively hated anything ugly ever since I was small.

Giles was to open a whole world of beauty to me which I did not know existed.

But for the moment I merely felt frightened because he was so insistent, and I really could not believe that he wanted me to go to London, nor did I imagine for one moment that Daddy would let me go.

We found Daddy in his study sitting at his desk sorting the money into little piles of copper and silver.

27

He didn't look up as I entered but merely said:

"I'm busy, Samantha, but you can bring me a cup of tea."

"I've brought you a visitor who wants to speak to you, Daddy," I answered.

He turned his head impatiently, but when he saw Giles looking so elegant and out of place in the shabby old study, he rose somewhat reluctantly to his feet.

"I am Giles Bariatinsky, and I am staying at the Castle," Giles said. "I want to have a talk with you, Vicar."

Daddy looked at me meaningfully and I turned towards the door.

"I would like Samantha to stay," Giles said.

I saw Daddy raise his eyebrows, surprised not only that Giles should want me to be present, but also that he had used my Christian name.

In Little Poolbrook we addressed people formally until we had known them for years.

"Do sit down, Mr. Bariatinsky," Daddy suggested after a moment.

Giles sat on the arm of a leather chair.

"I want to tell you, Vicar," he said, "that your daughter is one of the most beautiful young women I have seen for years, and she will be a sensation in the profession I envisage for her."

Poor Daddy looked absolutely astounded.

But Giles didn't give him time to get his breath; he just went on talking.

He explained that there was a demand for photogenic young women who could wear beautiful clothes, so that their pictures could appear in the glossy magazines.

There was also a great opening for them in modelling gowns for important dress-shows.

"Places like Molyneux, Revelle's and Hartnell's have their

own mannequins who are permanently on their staff," Giles explained, "but when they give one of their big Shows they take on more girls from outside."

He looked at me and went on:

"I run an Agency of my own. It is very exclusive and very expensive. At the moment, I have two models, both of them outstandingly beautiful in their own way, and they just cannot cope with the demand for their services. I therefore wish to employ your daughter."

Giles paused for breath, but Daddy could not get a word in edgeways.

"I'll pay her," Giles continued, "four pounds a week all the year round. But she will earn between ten and fifteen pounds quite easily doing outside work, of which she will keep fifty per cent."

Both Daddy and I gasped at that, which was not surprising, considering that his stipend was three hundred pounds a year, out of which he had to pay the rates of the Vicarage.

"Is that possible?" Daddy asked at last.

"That's a very conservative estimate of what your daughter could earn," Giles answered. "I visualise that in time Samantha will earn a great deal more. She will have expenses, of course."

"Where would she live?" my father asked rather limply.

I was surprised that he had not turned down the proposal out of hand. Then before Giles could answer he added sharply:

"It would be impossible, of course, for Samantha to live on her own. She is only eighteen and has always lived a very quiet and sheltered life."

"I can understand that . . ." Giles said.

"Therefore, in the circumstances," Daddy continued before Giles could go any further, "I'm afraid, Mr.

Bariatinsky, I must refuse your suggestion. I feel sure that if Samantha's mother was alive she would agree with me that London is not the right place for a young girl."

At that moment I had not made up my mind whether Giles's proposition was really genuine.

I could not help feeling that the whole thing was too incredible to be real.

He might have just invented it to make fun of us, or perhaps he really was mad, as I had at first thought.

But now I felt a definite tremor of regret that I could not go to London; that I would have to stay in Little Poolbrook wearing the wrong clothes and trimming for myself the wrong hats; and no-one ever again would call me beautiful.

But I didn't know Giles in those days. I had no idea that he always got his own way.

"I can quite understand your feelings, Vicar," he said in a conciliatory tone, "but don't you think you are being a little selfish?"

"Selfish?" Daddy ejaculated.

It was one of his fondest conceits that he was one of the most unselfish men alive.

Actually he always *was* thinking of other people.

"Call it chance, fate, or good fortune," Giles went on, "but you have an exceptionally beautiful child. Do you think it fair to the world that you should keep her entirely to yourself? That you should bury her, for that's what it amounts to, in this backwater?"

He paused to say slowly:

"Isn't it written somewhere in the Bible that you shouldn't hide your light under a bushel? Your achievement, Vicar, has been to produce one of the most exquisite creatures I have ever seen in the whole of my career!"

Well that, of course, clinched it.

They went on talking for a long time, but I could see that

30

Daddy was upset by the suggestion that he was being selfish and standing in my way, and Giles, having made his point, went on pressing it home until all Daddy's defences crumbled.

"Samantha shall be well looked after," Giles promised. "There is a Boarding House to which I have sent other girls. The Proprietress is a friend of mine and very strict. Anyway, I promise you, she will be working too hard to have time to get into any mischief."

This, I was to discover later, was one of Giles's pet convictions in which he actually believed.

But at this time Daddy and I were far too ignorant to contradict him or indeed to query anything he said.

Finally I heard my father say in a weak, somehow defenceless voice:

"When would you want Samantha to start work?"

"At once," Giles answered sharply. "This week at the latest. In fact I will take her back to London with me to-morrow night."

"It's impossible!" Daddy and I said simultaneously.

Then Giles began to sweep all our objections to one side, one after another, until finally we capitulated.

"I've no clothes," I murmured feebly when we had no more ammunition left.

"You certainly don't want to waste your money buying rubbish like that dress you are wearing at the moment," Giles said disparagingly. "I'll see you are properly fitted out as soon as we get to London."

He glanced scornfully at my green muslin and added:

"Once you have acquired some semblance of good taste, you'll find it quite easy to choose things for yourself."

I meekly accepted his sweeping condemnation of the new dress over which I had expended so much time and trouble.

I knew he was right!

31

At the same time it frightened me to think how much I had to learn.

I didn't realise then, as I realise now, how abysmally ignorant I was . . .

Reflection 4

Giles ought to be here at any moment, so I'll go into the Sitting-room to wait for him.

One advantage of having a flat on the ground floor is that one needn't keep waiting people who come to call and they do not have to come inside.

In fact the only person who has been in here for more than a moment or two is Peter, when he came to hang the pictures which came to London with the furniture from the Vicarage.

It is nice having around me the things I have known all my life although, of course, some of them are rather big, especially the mahogany bed-stead which fills the Bed-room at the back so that there is hardly room to move.

But I couldn't leave that bed behind. I had known it all my life. I was born in it for one thing, and I can remember when I was small creeping into Mummy's room innumerable times in the middle of the night and saying:

"There's a . . . ghost in my room . . . Mummy."

"Nonsense, Samantha! There are no such things."

She would speak in a whisper so as not to disturb Daddy who was asleep beside her.

"If it isn't a ghost . . . it's a very big . . . goblin. I can hear it."

"Now, darling, you know quite well that is only the water-pipes," Mummy would say.

"But I'm . . . frightened!"

That of course, meant that I could get into bed beside Mummy and Daddy and feel really safe.

I have never since felt so safe and secure as I did then.

Sometimes I wonder if I would feel like that if I was lying close to David. But I don't want to think about . . . that . . . I won't think about . . . it.

I'll just powder my nose and go to the window and see if there is any sign of Giles.

It doesn't really need any more powder. I remember David saying once:

"I adore your proud little nose, Samantha."

I felt myself thrill at his words. Then he added, and his voice changed to become mocking and rather sarcastic:

"Of course, it is straight and unbending like your principles which infuriate me!"

So instead of feeling happy and excited, I felt weak and deflated and wanted to cry!!

But all that is over. I'm going to be different now . . . at least, I hope I am!

There's no sign of Giles yet, but I'll wait just by the door so that I can hurry out to him the moment his car draws up outside.

I like so much being on my own and having my things around me, that I couldn't bear anyone to disparage them, which I am sure he will do.

I know the green carpet that was in Mummy's Drawing-room is rather worn and the flowery chintzes are a little faded, but they are part of me.

I love them, just as I love the marquetry china cabinet which Peter said was quite valuable, and Mummy's work-box which is Queen Anne and the battered tapestry chair Daddy always used.

I love these things because they are mine and they belong to me. I don't really care if Giles, or anyone else thinks they look old and shabby.

But I don't want them to say so in my hearing.

Oh, there he is! Now at last we can set off for this horrible party.

I wonder how soon I can get away. Giles is bound to want to stay to the bitter end. But there is sure to be someone else there who will give me a lift home.

Reflection 5

Giles is in one of his grumpier moods when he doesn't talk.

I'm glad because I've nothing to say.

His car is very comfortable. I always think that Hispano Suizas look romantic, but Bentleys are my favourite cars. All the smart young men have one, so that they are called 'The Bentley Boys'.

The first time I went out in a Bentley after coming to London, I felt terribly grand and rather dashing, and it was thrilling to rush along faster than I had ever travelled before.

But David's Bentley took us into a world of our own. It was a fiery chariot in which we could escape so that no-one knew where we were or could interrupt us.

It was a secret place made of dreams, a cloud on which we could float above the world and forget it ever existed.

It was a Heaven on wheels where I first knew what it meant to thrill and thrill and thrill . . .

Reflection 6

Everything in those first few weeks was overwhelming, simply because it was all new and I was continually being taken by surprise.

The first big surprise was that Daddy ever agreed that I should go to London, although two minutes after Giles had left us with a self-satisfied smirk on his face because he had got his own way, Daddy began to have misgivings.

"I hope I've done the right thing, Samantha," he kept saying.

When the bazaar was over we went home to eat a very nasty meat-pie that Mrs. Harris had left for us in a low oven, which was still too hot.

He sat at the table looking so worried that I said in a rather small voice:

"If you don't want me to go Daddy, I'll stay . . . here with you."

"No, Samantha," he answered, "I think you ought to go. That Mr. Bariatinsky is right when he says this is a chance for you to see the world and get away from Little Pool-brook."

"I'm not certain I want to get away from it," I said.

"Well, if you are not happy, you can always come home," he replied.

"Of course," I agreed, "and as soon as I make enough money we can put a new stove in the kitchen so that we shall not have to eat any more burnt pie-crust."

Daddy laughed at that, which was what I had intended.

But when we went to sit in the study he fidgeted about, which I knew meant he had something on his mind.

After a little while he said:

"I wish your mother was here to have a talk with you, Samantha."

"What about?" I asked.

"About going to London," Daddy replied. "You do realise my dear, that there will be a lot of difficulties and temptations which you haven't encountered before?"

"What sort of temptations?" I asked curiously.

Daddy didn't look at me and I knew he was embarrassed.

"For one thing you are very pretty, Samantha," he said. "And I expect there will be plenty of young men to tell you so."

"Surely there is nothing wrong in that?" I asked.

"No, of course not," he agreed, "but I don't want you to lose your head and behave in a manner your mother wouldn't have liked."

"I see no reason why I should do that," I answered. "I always try to do things in the way Mummy would have approved."

"Yes, I know that," Daddy answered. "You are a good child, Samantha, but it may be very different in London."

He said it in such a worried manner that I couldn't help feeling he was keeping something from me.

"What are you trying to say, Daddy?" I asked.

"I am only trying to warn you," he answered. "It is very easy, I believe, for young girls to be led astray, especially if they are pretty."

"Do you mean that men would make ... love to me?" I asked.

There was a pause and then Daddy said:

"I'm hoping, Samantha, that one day you will fall in love with someone, get married and be really happy, just as your mother and I were. As you know, she had many opportunities to marry far more important and richer men than me; but as soon as we met, we knew we were meant for each other."

"I should like that to happen to me," I said.

"I hope it will," Daddy answered. "I shall pray it will, Samantha. But I want you to keep yourself for the one man who will matter in your life."

"I promise you one thing, Daddy," I answered, "I would never think of marrying anyone that I didn't love."

"I hope not," Daddy answered. "At the same time, men don't always offer – marriage."

I thought about this for a moment and then I said:

"You mean they might want to kiss me and not be really seriously in love?"

"Something like that," Daddy answered.

"Well, I expect I shall know if they are genuinely fond of me or not," I said lightly. "Don't worry about me. I'm sure I will be able to take care of myself."

I really believed I could do that, until I got to London and realised how big and overwhelming it was.

It made me feel very small and insignificant.

Giles drove me up, but he didn't say very much on the way and he took me straight to the Boarding House he had talked about, which was in South Kensington.

The Proprietress, who obviously was very impressed by him, was a middle-aged woman with a rather severe appearance, but she was very gushing when Giles explained that he had brought her a new boarder.

"Miss Clyde is from the country," he said. "I promised her father, who is a Clergyman, that you would look after her and see that she doesn't get into any trouble."

"No, of course she won't, Mr. Bariatinsky," Mrs. Simpson said positively. "She'll be very happy here in this friendly little community, which is how I always think of my guests."

When Giles had gone she took me upstairs and showed me a very small, ugly back room which she informed me I could have for twenty-five shillings a week with breakfast.

"Supper is extra," she said. "I expect all my boarders to be out for lunch. Most of them work, like yourself."

She showed me where the bathroom was on a half-landing and told me I must pay sixpence every time I used it. Then she said:

"There is a lounge where you can entertain your friends, but you must understand that friends are not allowed in your Bed-room."

She said 'friends' in rather a strange voice and I thought it was most unlikely that anyone would want to visit me in such a bare and cheerless place. But I didn't say so and after a moment Mrs. Simpson went on in a more severe tone:

"What's more, I don't expect gentlemen to be entertained in the lounge after ten o'clock. Is that quite clear?"

"Yes, of course," I answered. "But as I don't know anyone in London, I think it is unlikely that I shall have anyone coming to see me here."

She gave me a hard look as if she thought I was deceiving her and then she went downstairs to tell the porter to bring up my luggage.

I unpacked and went to bed. I must admit that, lying on the hard mattress in the dark, I suddenly felt homesick and wished I had never set out on this adventure.

I felt I would much rather be in my own comfortable little bed, knowing there was nothing more alarming to think about to-morrow than getting up in time to prepare Daddy's breakfast and clear up the mess that had been left in the house after the bazaar.

I suddenly felt the whole thing was ridiculous.

How could I, ordinary little Samantha Clyde, expect that anyone in London would think me attractive, let alone beautiful? I was quite certain that when Giles developed the photographs he had taken of me he would find I looked hideous.

In fact I felt thoroughly depressed.

Reflection 7

The next few days were awful.

I went to Giles's studio first thing in the morning, as he had told me to do and was introduced to his secretary, Miss Macey, a thin, plain, rather bossy woman with glasses, who spoke to Giles in one voice and to me and the other models in quite a different tone.

She always appeared to despise us, but Melanie and Hortense told me later that it was because she was madly in love with Giles and couldn't bear any other woman to go near him.

She always did exactly what he told her. When she was sent out to bring back the clothes he thought I should have, I must say everything she produced was absolutely lovely.

It would have been difficult to find fault with any of them.

Melanie had fair golden hair and a baby face, so that she looked very young and almost like an angel off a Christmas tree.

She looked absolutely wonderful in the photographs Giles had taken of her in dresses for young girls, but she had a sharp tongue and was at times quite vitriolic.

Hortense, on the other hand, was a brunette and, I thought, very attractive, but far too lazy to be cross or disagreeable with anyone. All she wanted to do was sleep.

"I'm dead on my feet!" she would say every morning when she arrived, and at every opportunity would flop down into a chair and shut her eyes. It made Giles simply furious.

I found there were all sorts of extra little jobs we were expected to do while we were waiting in the studio for him to photograph us.

We had to sort out prints, help Miss Macey pack them up, answer the telephone and do all sorts of things which, as Melanie complained continually, were not really part of our job.

I didn't mind, but Melanie said that Giles was a slave-driver determined to have his 'pound of flesh' one way or another, because it annoyed him that we earned so much money outside and he had to give us fifty per cent.

But he was very kind to me over my clothes.

I paid for some of them and the rest he allowed me to put down as a debt against my wages.

For the first time I had money of my own and thought I was enormously rich!

Just before Giles called for me at the Vicarage on Sunday evening, Daddy gave me five pounds in notes and a cheque for another fifteen pounds.

"You can't spare all that!" I said in astonishment.

"I don't want you to feel penniless, Samantha," he answered, "and you are always to leave yourself enough money for your railway-ticket home."

"But I can't spend twenty pounds!" I exclaimed.

"You'll find it won't go far in London," he said dryly.

"But how can you afford to give me so much?"

"I have a little 'nest-egg' in the bank against a rainy day," he said, "and I think to-day is definitely a storm."

I knew he was trying to put a cheerful face on the fact that I was going away, and he was still worried about me.

So I laughed, hugged him and promised I would pay it all back as soon as I was raking in the millions that Giles had said I would make.

"I want you to have a good time," Daddy said. "I realise now how dull it must have been for you here in Little Pool-brook, and I am afraid I forgot how young you were, Sam-antha, or rather that you are old enough to want something more amusing than parochial tea parties."

"If you talk like that you'll make me cry," I said. "I have been happy, terribly happy, and I don't really want to go away at all. In fact, don't be surprised if I'm back next week!"

"Give it a proper trial, Samantha," he said. "But if anything goes wrong, promise you will come home."

"Wrong?" I asked, "what do you mean by wrong?"

"If you are – unhappy," Daddy answered, "or if you lose your job."

I had a feeling that that was not all he envisaged might happen, but I couldn't imagine what he was trying to say. So we just waited almost in silence until Giles arrived.

I had no idea until I got to London how important a professional Giles was.

There was no doubt that he had a name to conjure with, as they say.

"Are you really a 'Giles Bariatinsky model'?" people would say to me at parties, or: "I might have guessed that Giles Bariatinsky would want to photograph you – he will only do beautiful women."

There was a legend which I found to be untrue, that women who were ugly would offer him a blank cheque to take pictures of them, and he would wave them away disdainfully.

Actually he posed them against the most amazing and fantastic settings so that their ugliness was lost in their surroundings. And when the photographs were developed, he touched them up.

He was really an artist and he did it so cleverly that he could produce quite lovely photographs of women described by Melanie as having faces 'like the back of a cab'.

Of course, they were delighted and would pay astronomical sums to have dozens of prints of each pose to give to their friends.

I soon found out that sitting for Giles was hard work.

The lighting was very hot and he would take one pose for hours on end until he was satisfied he had got exactly what he wanted.

It was almost as tiring as the dress-shows.

I had always imagined from the magazines that the girls who wore the dresses of the famous couturiers had a marvellous time.

I was to find it was just sheer hard work.

One would have to put on perhaps twenty dresses for a show, and then when it was over put them on over and over again for first one customer and then another.

Funnily enough, it was Miss Macey who taught me how to walk when I was modelling gowns.

I learnt there were training-schools for mannequins, but Giles thought they were just a waste of money.

"If you are naturally graceful, as you are, Samantha," he said, "you only have to learn a few tricks like holding yourself correctly, moving your feet in the right manner, and knowing what to do with your hands."

It all sounded quite easy, but it took hours and hours of walking up and down the studio floor, backwards and forwards, turning, smiling, turning again, walking backwards, until Miss Macey, and then Giles, were satisfied.

They made me feel gauche and clumsy, but Hortense told me she had taken far longer to learn what they wanted and that at one time Giles had considered sacking her because she was slow.

That made me feel better, but when I saw Melanie and Hortense in the first show we all did together, I realised how graceful they were, and how they made every dress they put on seem a dream of elegance.

I soon learnt also that we didn't work only in the day-time, but in the evening too.

Giles's models were expected to appear at cocktail parties wearing dresses which were written about in the newspapers, so that they could be ordered by the smart socialites who admired them.

When some of the men who talked to us at cocktail parties asked us out to dinner, Melanie and Hortense made it quite clear that we were expected to accept their invitations.

I found that the clothes Giles chose for me had all come from famous houses: Pacquin, Revelle, Molyneux and Hartnell.

These were, of course, last season's models which they were prepared to dispose of for a few pounds. But they still had that indefinable chic which made people look at me when I walked into a restaurant or appeared at a cocktail party.

For very special occasions we borrowed the current models from the same places.

I found that extremely nerve-racking. I was so afraid the dress would get torn or that I would upset something on it, that I could not enjoy the evening because I was worrying all the time about my clothes.

Hortense told me a terrifying story of how a young man had upset a glass of wine on a white dress she was wearing, and when the shop it had come from made her pay for it, it had taken her four months before she was out of debt.

That story did nothing to reassure me and I was more nervous than ever.

In fact I hated having to borrow a special gown, but Giles got quite angry when he thought I didn't look spectacular enough.

His photographs of me were certainly fabulous.

It was very exciting when I saw them for the first time in *Vogue* and Miss Macey told me in a condescending way that there was already quite a demand from other magazines and newspapers for my pictures.

I thought at first of sending copies back to Daddy to show

him how marvellous I looked, but then I was afraid it might upset him.

I didn't really look a bit like myself.

I looked alluring and mysterious, exotic and sophisticated, and sometimes rather fast and improper.

The young men who took me out in the evening nearly always gave me orchids because they said it was the flower I most resembled.

Personally I have always thought that orchids are overrated; they have no smell and there is something rather unfriendly about them.

Of course I couldn't say so, and at first I used to put them painstakingly in a vase when I got home and tried to keep them alive. But in the end I would throw them away, and when I could afford it, I'd buy myself a few roses from the barrow at the bottom of the street.

I can't remember now, looking back, who was the first man to try to kiss me when taking me home from a party.

All the young men in the Brigade of Guards thought it smart to be seen with the 'Giles Bariatinsky models'.

Melanie and Hortense introduced me to some of them and they in their turn introduced me to their friends, so that I found within a week or so I knew quite a number of men in London.

At first I felt shy of dining alone with a man and much preferred it when they asked Melanie or Hortense to make it a foursome. But one night a young man whom Melanie rather fancied obviously preferred me, and she was furious.

After that the girls wouldn't make up a four, and so it was a case of either going out alone or staying in the Boarding House. That was so depressing that I would have done anything to get away.

Anyway, whoever took me out always seemed to think he must try to kiss me. I was surprised since I had always expected to know a man a long time before he tried to kiss me.

If my dinner host was driving his own car, he would wait until we drew up outside the Boarding House which looked dark and unwelcoming in the early hours of the morning.

Then he would put an arm round my shoulders and begin:

"You are very lovely, Samantha!"

I grew very adroit at opening the door of the car just as my escort put on the brakes and I would therefore be out on the pavement before he could realise what was happening.

"Good-night!" I would say.

"Wait, Samantha, wait!" he would call as he jumped out of the other side of the car.

He would catch up with me just as I reached the front door and had my finger on the bell.

"Aren't you going to say good-night to me?" he would ask.

"Not here," I would answer quickly.

Sometimes the porter, who was very old, which was why Mrs. Simpson got him cheap, would take some time to shuffle across the Hall. Then I would have to twist myself away and struggle a little, but I was always rescued just in time by the door opening.

"Good-night, and thank you so much!" I'd say, and slip inside before he could do anything more about it.

It was rather more difficult in a taxi, because a taxi door is harder to open from the inside.

But a man who brought me home in a taxi was, I found, not so dashing or so sure of himself as the ones who owned cars – especially Bentleys.

He would usually begin with:

"Please let me kiss you, Samantha."

"No," I'd reply. "I don't want to be kissed."

"You can't expect me to believe that," he would protest. "Say yes, Samantha, just this once."

There was sometimes a little struggle, but I always managed to avoid being kissed, simply because I didn't want to
be . . . until I met David.

Oh, dear, I don't want to think about that . . . but I can't
help it. It's engraved on my heart like 'Calais' on Queen
Mary's . . . that wonderful, magical, unforgettable kiss . . .

Reflection 8

Here we are at the Meldriths' grand house in Grosvenor
Square and I only hope she won't ask me if I've seen David
lately.

Lady Meldrith may well connect us together considering I
met him at one of her parties.

But perhaps she won't remember that, and now I think
about it, there is really no reason why she should give
another thought to what happened in June.

Out of all the people Lady Meldrith has entertained why
should she recall the first time she entertained me?

Of course she has asked me to dinner twice since I came
back to London, and each time I've chucked her at the last
moment.

I just couldn't face the house and all the memories it has
for me! But I'm sure Lady Meldrith only asked me because I
am a 'Giles Bariatinsky model'.

How well I remember this Hall. It impressed me the first
time I came here.

The Meldriths must be extremely rich. I think in fact he is
one of the Captains of Industry, or something like that.

The marble statues are lovely. Peter would appreciate

those, but, of course, he must have seen them. I am sure the Meldriths have had everything in this house valued by Christies at some time or another.

The staff look very snooty and bored.

If I ever entertain I shall tell my servants to look welcoming and pleasant when people arrive.

It puts me off a party from the very beginning if the servants appear to find you a nuisance the moment that you are in through the door. But I suppose the sort of people the Meldriths entertain don't care what servants think, one way or another.

I doubt if they even think of them as people.

Lady Meldrith is what they call 'Café Society'. She mixes with the grand and the notorious, the famous and the infamous. That sounds frightfully clever, but I didn't think of it myself. I heard somebody say it about her and I thought it amusing.

Reflection 9

It was obvious that Lady Meldrith would invite David to her parties the moment his book made him the most talked-of young man in London.

I had heard of him simply because everybody was arguing about *Vultures Pick Their Bones*.

It was a strange, rather creepy title and it seemed to be on everybody's tongue.

Pacquin had a dress they called 'The Vulture' after David's book was serialised in one of the Sunday papers, and the critics worked themselves up into a frenzy, half-praising and half-criticising it.

I remember Giles telling Miss Macey to try to get David to come and be photographed.

"Do you know where he lives?" Miss Macey had asked.

"I've no idea," Giles replied. "Look in the telephone book, or try the clubs. He's sure to be a member of White's or Boodle's."

"I've seen a photograph of him somewhere," Melanie said. "I think it was by Dorothy Wilding."

She only said that to annoy Giles, who was jealous of Dorothy Wilding, especially when she photographed the people he wanted to do.

"Get hold of David Durham and do it quickly!" he ordered Miss Macey.

"If he's the sort of young man I think he is," Miss Macey retorted, "it's unlikely he'll want to sit for a studio portrait."

"According to Melanie, he has already had one taken," Giles answered.

He looked at Melanie in a searching sort of way as he spoke and she said uneasily:

"I may have been mistaken. It might have been somebody else or an ordinary press photograph."

I wasn't really listening to the conversation at the time because I wasn't interested in David Durham. But because Giles was making such a fuss about him, I said to Miss Macey when he had gone:

"Who is this writer?"

"He's one of the so-called 'Flaming Youth'," she answered. "His first two books made a bit of a stir but nothing compared to this one. You'd think he was leading a crusade instead of tearing everybody and everything to bits in a book!"

She was obviously so irritable about having to try to find David Durham that I didn't ask her any more.

I certainly never expected to meet him.

Although I had been about quite a lot during the short time I had been in London, I hadn't met anyone of any importance.

They were nearly all very young men who wanted to dance and drive fast cars and who talked incessantly about being 'on guard' and 'on parade' and what the Colonel had said in the Mess.

They were very gay and I enjoyed dancing with them, but no-one, not even the Vicar's daughter of Little Poolbrook, would have thought them intellectual.

I thought to myself that David Durham sounded pretty terrifying, but it was very unlikely that I should ever meet him, even if he came to be photographed. If he did, I was quite certain that Melanie would contrive to monopolise him.

Melanie had a way of always getting what she wanted.

She had been determined to go in a smart party to Ascot. She talked about it all the week beforehand and was furious that no-one had asked her.

However there was an impecunious Baronet who had been hanging around and somehow through him she managed to meet Lord Rowden, and came back absolutely delighted with herself.

"He's taking a large party," she said, "and we are going down in a coach – think of that! He'll have all sorts of rich and exciting guests, and I've got to have something very special to wear."

"You'd better be careful of that gentleman," Miss Macey said rather sourly.

"Why?" Melanie asked briefly.

"You'll soon find out," Miss Macey replied.

"I assure you that I can take care of myself," Melanie said with an edge on her voice.

"I'm sure you *think* you can," Miss Macey replied nastily.

There was no love lost between Miss Macey and the models, but I never argued with her.

I couldn't bear even to hear the spiteful remarks that she and Melanie made to each other, let alone utter them.

But Melanie had got her own way and she went down to Ascot with her smart party and came back having had, according to her, a fabulous time and won over twenty pounds on the races.

"It's easy to win when you don't stake your own money," Miss Macey said.

"Who'd be stupid enough to do that?" Melanie enquired, putting on her innocent look!

It was the week of the Ascot races that the Meldriths gave one of their much publicised parties and invited Giles to bring one of his models with him.

On that occasion the party was not given for anyone special and he decided to take me because Melanie was not available and they had seen Hortense before.

"You'll want a special cocktail dress," he said. "Better go along to Pacquin and ask them to lend you something out-standing. A Meldrith party is one of the best advertising mediums in London."

Obediently I trotted off to Pacquin and when I explained what Giles had said they produced the most fantastic outfit. It was in silver lamé with an emerald-green and silver turban to wear on my head and huge imitation emerald ear-rings which were part of the get-up.

It seemed to me to be completely fancy-dress and I felt very outré and rather shy in it, but Giles was delighted.

"I'll photograph you in it before you send it back to-morrow," he said, "it's just the sort of picture *Vogue* likes."

But even his enthusiasm didn't make me feel any less con-spicuous as I walked up the Meldriths' grand staircase into the huge double Drawing-room on the first floor.

Although we were fairly early it seemed to be packed with people and the noise was deafening.

There was a Band and where there were a few inches of room on the parquet floor people were dancing.

There never seemed to be a time of day in London when people were not dancing. There were even newspaper reports of people dancing at breakfast-time.

I myself never saw anyone at breakfast except the other boarders in Mrs. Simpson's house, most of whom were not the type to dance at any time of the day.

The Bright Young People beloved of the gossip-columns apparently danced from the time they got up until the time they went to bed.

I had never been asked to dance before the evening because I was at work all day, but Hortense told me she had been taken several times to tea-dances at the Savoy Hotel and said they were very smart.

Anyway the Band, which consisted of a piano, a saxophone and a drum, was playing softly at one end of the Drawing-room.

People were dancing with cocktail glasses in their hands which made me at once feel nervous about my borrowed Pacquin gown.

If I looked strange all in silver lamé, the hem of my gown ballooning out like huge Eastern trousers, to be caught at the ankle with emerald buttons, there were other people looking just as strange, including a woman with a whole bird of Paradise on her head.

Lady Meldrith, who is small, vivacious and looks rather like a pretty parakeet, greeted Giles effusively and said:

"Oh, I'm so glad you've brought your new girl with you. I've been longing to see her. Those photographs in *Vogue* are too, too divine!"

"You flatter me," Giles replied with delight.

"I could never do that," Lady Meldrith answered with a

meaningful look of her eyes under mascara-ed eye-lashes.

Giles kissed her hand and then other guests arrived and we moved further into the room.

I looked round. The women were all terribly smart, sleekly brittle types with bored expressions, and the men seemed older and rather heavy, as if weighed down with their money.

Giles, of course, knew lots of people, and he was soon surrounded by women begging him to photograph them, saying they would die of shame if he refused.

Since nobody seemed interested in me, I edged my way towards a window at the end of the further room.

I found it looked out on to a very elaborate formal roof-garden.

There were brilliant flowers, including lilies which I love, a small fountain and seats arranged under orange trees planted in pots.

There was nobody in the garden and so, hoping no-one would notice, I walked down the steps from the Reception-room and stood looking at the lilies.

I hadn't been there more than a moment when a man and a woman came down the steps behind me.

I moved as far away as I could from them but it was impossible not to overhear their conversation.

"You said you'd telephone me last night, Ralph," the woman said petulantly.

"I'm sorry, Elsie, I got back too late from the races."

"I waited for hours because I wanted to talk to you."

"I thought you would be sure to be out and enjoying yourself."

"That is untrue, and you know it. How can you treat me like this? You know how I feel about you."

"Oh, for God's sake, Elsie, don't make a scene here."

"I don't get much chance of making one anywhere else, do I?"

The woman's voice rose a little.

I felt, although I had my back to them, that the man was looking in my direction and feeling embarrassed.

"When can I see you?" Elsie asked almost desperately.

"I have no idea," the man answered indifferently. "Sometime, I dare say."

The woman made an exasperated sound which was half-angry and half-tearful. Then as if she could not control herself, she turned and ran up the steps and back into the crowded Drawing-room.

I stood staring at the flowers and hoping the man would follow her, but he walked across the roof-garden to my side.

"I know who you are," he said, "so may I introduce myself?"

I turned and saw he was heavily built and much older than I had thought. He had rather a dissipated look but he might have been handsome in his twenties.

"Your face has haunted me ever since I first saw a picture of you," he said. "My name is Rowden – Ralph Rowden."

"How do you do?" I said, rather nervously.

"I had one of the girls who work with you in my party at Ascot yesterday," he said.

"Yes, of course," I answered. "Melanie told us you had invited her."

"I am sure she enjoyed herself," he said. "Why don't you come down with me to-morrow?"

"No, thank you," I said quickly, "I'm afraid I have another engagement."

I had been in trouble with Melanie already because one of her young men took a fancy to me. I certainly didn't want to be involved in another row, even though Lord Rowden was not a man you could call 'young'.

In fact I thought he must be nearly forty.

"Let us sit down and discuss it," he said. "I'm sure, like me, you dislike this noisy party."

"I hate cocktail parties," I answered. "They always seem so pointless."

"I can think of a far better way for us to get acquainted," he said. "A quiet little dinner where we can talk."

I didn't know what to answer to that so I merely looked away across the roofs.

"What are you thinking, Samantha?" he asked.

I thought it was great cheek of him to call me by my Christian name, but I didn't quite see how I could stop him.

"I was wondering how soon I could leave," I answered.

Lord Rowden laughed.

"That's not very complimentary—unless you're suggesting that you and I should leave together."

"No, of course not!" I said quickly. "I am here with Giles Bariatinsky and he will take me home."

"I would like to do that," Lord Rowden said, "but as it happens, I cannot ask you to dine with me to-night as I already have an engagement which I cannot break. What about to-morrow night?"

I suddenly knew that I didn't wish to dine with him alone. There was something in the way he looked at me; something which made me feel uncomfortable and shy. I had felt shy with other people, but this was a different feeling.

"I . . . I . . . think it is . . . impossible."

"Nothing is impossible," he answered. "Not where you and I are concerned."

I rose to my feet.

"I must go and find Giles," I said. "He will be very annoyed with me for disappearing. I only came out here for a breath of air."

"I'll let you go, as long as you promise that you will dine with me to-morrow night," Lord Rowden said.

I was about to refuse again, and then I thought of a better idea.

"May I let you know in the morning?" I asked. "I could telephone and leave a message with your secretary."

"If you ring before eleven o'clock you can talk to me," he said, "or better still, I will telephone you."

"It might be difficult to find me," I said evasively. "I'll telephone you – I promise."

"Are you a truthful person, Samantha?" he asked.

"Yes, of course," I answered.

"There is no 'of course' about it," he replied. "Most women lie like hell! But funnily enough, I believe you, and if you say you will telephone, you will. What is more, Samantha, I will not take 'no' for an answer."

I was walking towards the steps all the time we were talking and now I climbed up them and saw to my relief that Giles was just a little way inside the window.

"I'll telephone you before eleven o'clock to-morrow," I said to Lord Rowden, and moved quickly to Giles's side.

He took no notice of me because he was deep in conversation, but the young man he was talking to looked at me and said:

"Won't you introduce us?"

Giles glanced in my direction almost as if he had forgotten that I existed.

"Yes, of course! Samantha, this is the famous young writer, whom everyone is talking about and who has confounded all the critics by his unprecedented success. David Durham – Samantha Clyde!"

He was not in the least what I had expected.

For one thing he was taller and more broad-shouldered than I had, perhaps stupidly, expected a writer to be.

He was also very smart with that easy elegance with which Englishmen can wear their clothes, and make them seem a part of themselves.

He had dark, penetrating eyes under winged eye-brows, and a mouth which seemed to have a cynical twist to it.

It was a strange face, almost sardonic, and it had a mocking, somewhat raffish look, as if he was prepared to dare anything and laugh at himself while he did so.

He held my hand for what seemed to me to be a fraction longer than was necessary and then – I don't know how it happened – Giles seemed to move away and we were in a corner of the room, David Durham and I, with a cocktail I didn't want in my hand.

"Tell me about yourself," he said.

"There's nothing to tell," I answered. "You are the one who has a lot to say."

It must have seemed quite a sophisticated, amusing retort, because he laughed.

"What I said in my book had to be said, sooner or later," he explained. "I was just fortunate to be the first one to say it."

As I had not read his book, and had not the slightest idea what it was about, I was not certain what to reply, so I merely asked:

"Do you enjoy being a success?"

"Enormously," he answered. "Don't you?"

"I'm not a success, as myself," I answered, "but because I am a 'Giles Bariatinsky model'. That's a very different thing. I haven't achieved anything."

"Except an unforgettable face," he answered.

"I think that is a compliment to my father and mother."

"I'll send them a bouquet to-morrow," he answered.

"Make it of ever-greens!"

It seemed to me that I had never been able to talk so lightly or gaily to anyone before.

It was almost like drinking champagne and feeling it go to one's head.

We talked for what must have been a long time and then he said:

"Let's go somewhere more comfortable. I always talk best with my elbows on a table."

I looked at him tentatively.

"I'm suggesting," he said as if I had asked him a question, "that you should come out to dinner with me."

"I don't think I . . . ought to," I said a little nervously.

"I never do things I ought to do," David answered. "I do what I want, and I most positively and definitely want to be with you, Samantha."

I knew then that I had no choice in the matter.

I just had to do what David wanted.

Reflection 10

Nothing I had ever known in my whole life had prepared me for David Durham.

I suppose, like all lonely children, I had invented a fantasy world of my own which had gradually evolved into the love-imaginings of an adolescent.

I had expected men to be strong and masculine, authoritative but tender, and rather respectful where women were concerned.

Of course, I must have based my conception of a man in love on the way my father treated my mother, and his obvious adoration of her.

I had never imagined that anyone could be as vitally and irresistibly attractive as David Durham.

He took me to a small, quiet restaurant where there were very few other people. The head waiter was pleased to see him and we were shown to a secluded sofa-table in an alcove.

He ordered food for both of us and I was given champagne, although I didn't ask for it.

Then David put his elbows on the table and talked.

I can't remember now what we talked about. I only knew it was fascinatingly exciting, and I must have sat like a mesmerised rabbit with my eyes on his face, trying to understand what he was saying to me.

But of course, I didn't look stupid, ignorant and bemused, as I in fact felt inside. I looked enigmatic, exotic and doubtless very sophisticated in the silver lamé with the long emerald ear-rings swinging against my white skin.

When dinner was finished a man started to play the piano very softly at the other end of the room.

David got to his feet and said:

"I want to dance with you, Samantha."

When he put his arms round me I felt a strange feeling in my throat. I couldn't explain it; at the same time it was wildly exciting.

He held me very close and although there were only two or three other couples on the floor he moved very slowly in the manner of people who dance when there is hardly room to move.

"I like your scent," he said, after a moment.

It was difficult for me to remember what it was.

At the shops where we gave dress-shows they often had their own make of scent and sometimes, if they were feeling generous, they gave us a small bottle, hoping we would recommend it.

I thought I might be wearing one of Molyneux's but I wasn't really certain. When I was dressing I used the first bottle that came to hand.

"I'm glad," I said after a moment.

"Are you?" David asked. "Are you really glad, Samantha,

that I should like your scent, and everything else about you?"

"You don't know me well enough to say that," I answered.

At the same time I felt very thrilled at his words. I wanted him to like me.

He was quite the most exciting person I had met since I came to London. At the same time he frightened me.

He knew so much. He seemed so sophisticated that I felt it was only a question of time, perhaps an hour or so, before he would realise how little there was about me to get to know and how inadequate I was in every way to be his companion even for dinner.

As we left the Meldriths I had told Giles we were leaving.

When he saw who I was with there had been a look of amusement on his face.

I thought perhaps it was because he thought that there was something incongruous about me, the girl he had discovered in Little Poolbrook wearing the wrong sort of clothes, going out with someone as famous as David Durham.

"You are a very mysterious person," David was saying in my ear as we moved slowly round the polished floor. "What are you thinking about behind that Sphinx-like expression in your eyes?"

I had heard this type of remark before from other men, but somehow it had quite a different significance when David said it.

But I was too nervous of giving him the wrong answer to reply. When I didn't say anything he gave a little laugh, held me tighter and said:

"Never mind. You are throwing me a challenge to discover your secrets for myself, and that is exactly what I want to do."

We went back to the table and talked, or at least he did,

until there was practically no-one left in the restaurant.

So he paid the bill and we went outside and got into his Bentley.

"Where do you want to go now?" he asked.

"I think I ought to go to bed," I answered. "I have a lot of work to do to-morrow morning."

I said it reluctantly because the last thing I wanted was to leave David Durham. But I expected he too, had been busy all day and I knew it was wiser for me to leave when he was still wanting me to stay than for him later to long to be rid of me.

"Where do you live?" he asked.

I gave him the address in South Kensington.

"You have a flat?" he enquired.

"No," I answered. "I live in a Boarding House."

"Can I come in and have a good-night drink?"

"No, you can't," I replied. "Mrs. Simpson has very strict rules and one is that we mustn't invite a man into the lounge after ten o'clock."

"I wasn't particularly interested in the lounge," David replied.

He spoke in a tone of voice which sounded as if he meant me to laugh, but I didn't really see it was funny.

After we had driven a little way I realised we were down by the river. He drove along the Embankment, then stopped between two street lights.

There was the water on one side of us and trees on the other. It was very quiet.

"Why are we stopping here?" I asked.

He didn't answer. Instead he put his arm round the back of the seat and pulled me towards him. I was so surprised that I made no effort to stop him and then his mouth was on mine.

It was the first time I had been kissed and for one second I thought it was disappointing.

His lips seemed hard and not what I had expected; then something wonderful happened inside me.

I can't really explain what it was like. It was so strange, and yet so utterly and completely marvellous.

It was like feeling very warm and weak and sort of melting away. Then it became a kind of thrill that went on and on! It was so exciting, so absolutely, unbelievably lovely, that I couldn't have moved even if I had wanted to.

I had never known I could feel like that!

I had no idea that a kiss was all the beautiful thoughts and feelings one had ever had rolled into one.

It was like looking at a perfect view, being utterly happy and at the same time feeling fireworks going off inside one.

It's no use trying to explain. It must be, I thought, what people meant by ecstasy – a word I had never understood before.

Then, when I wanted David to go on kissing me for ever, he suddenly took his arm away, started up the car without saying a word, and drove me back to the Boarding House so quickly that the Bentley seemed to skid round the corners.

When we got there I just sat rather stupidly looking at him.

He put his hand over mine and said in what I thought was a strange voice:

"Thank you, Samantha. I will pick you up to-morrow evening at eight o'clock."

He got out his side of the car, walked round, opened my door and took my arm to help me up the steps.

He rang the bell and for once the old porter opened the door quickly.

I walked in, and as I did so David turned away and walked back down the steps to his car.

Only when he had gone did I realise I had not said a word – I just hadn't had anything to say!

I went up to my room, took off my Pacquin dress, hanging it up carefully, and only when I was in my nightgown did I look at my face in the mirror to see if I had altered in any way.

I wouldn't have been surprised if I had looked quite different because I knew quite unmistakably that I was completely and irrevocably in love.

Reflection 11

I don't remember very much about the next day.

I do remember that before I left the Boarding House that morning I telephoned Lord Rowden's house.

He had said that if I rang early he would answer the telephone himself; but I knew I couldn't speak to him at the Studio because of Melanie, so I decided to pretend to be a servant speaking for me.

However there was no need to do that because when I looked in the telephone book I saw he had three telephone lines and one had 'Secretary' against it.

So I rang that number and when a woman answered, I said:

"Will you please give Lord Rowden a message?"

"Who is speaking?" she enquired.

"I am speaking for Miss Samantha Clyde," I replied. "Will you tell Lord Rowden that Miss Clyde is very sorry, but she is unable to dine with him to-night?"

With that I put the receiver down quickly, and hurried off to the Studio.

"Did you enjoy yourself last night?" Giles asked as soon as he came in, about an hour after we had all been waiting for him.

"Yes, thank you," I answered.

"I hope you persuaded David Durham to have his picture taken."

I felt rather guilty because I hadn't thought about Giles or his photographs all the evening.

I didn't answer for a moment, and Giles, realising it had escaped my memory, said sharply:

"You might remember, Samantha, that it is part of your job to bring in customers and I particularly want to photograph David Durham."

"I'll do what I can," I said meekly.

"Then you're seeing him again?"

"Yes," I answered.

Giles gave me a sharp glance, but he didn't ask any more questions and merely said:

"Good!" and started arranging the lights.

I never knew a day to pass so slowly.

It seemed to me as if every hour crawled past and I must have looked at the clock a hundred times to find it had only moved by a few minutes.

Giles kept me later that afternoon than Melanie and Hortense.

He had a number of photographs to do for a French magazine, but unfortunately he did the day-dresses first and the evening-gowns last, and nearly all my pictures were in evening dress.

At last when it was after six o'clock he finished, and I was just hurrying into my own clothes when the telephone on Miss Macey's desk rang.

Only a curtain separated the place where we changed and the outer office, so I heard her say:

63

"Oh, yes, Lord Rowden, I'll try to find out."

She put her hand over the mouthpiece and as I looked round the curtain she said:

"Lord Rowden wants to know if I will give him your address."

My first thought was it was a blessing that Melanie had already gone home, and then I knew that I had no wish to see Lord Rowden again, or have anything to do with him.

"Tell him you don't know," I whispered.

"He won't believe that," Miss Macey replied.

"Then make some excuse; I don't want him ringing me at the Boarding House."

Miss Macey gave me a look to see if I was telling her the truth and then she said into the receiver:

"I'm so sorry but I believe Miss Clyde has recently changed her address and we don't seem to have it. But she'll be here to-morrow."

She put the receiver down and I said:

"Thank you. But if he rings again, what are you going to say?"

"I'll try to keep him away from you," Miss Macey said in a kinder tone than she usually used. "He's always running after pretty girls."

"But he's quite old," I exclaimed.

"Age doesn't stop them," Miss Macey remarked.

"Hasn't he got a wife?" I enquired.

"Oh, yes, and quite a number of children," Miss Macey replied. "Lady Rowden lives in Paris most of the time and I expect the children are at school or at his house in the country."

"Now I think of it," I said, "I seem to have seen some pictures somewhere of Rowden Park."

"It's one of the most famous houses in England," Miss Macey said, "but if you are wise, Samantha, you will leave His Lordship to Melanie. She should be able to cope with him."

64

"I think he's horrid and I don't want to see him again," I said.

For the first time I had known her, Miss Macey smiled and said to me pleasantly:

"Sometimes you make a lot of sense, Samantha."

I didn't think about Lord Rowden again. I was in such a hurry to get back and change.

I had to wait ages for a bus. Even so, having hurried to have a bath, I was ready for a good quarter of an hour before David arrived.

After the fantastic outfit I had worn the night before, I was determined to look quite different. So I put on a black dress that Giles had chosen for me, which I knew made my hair look fiery and my skin very white.

Made of black chiffon, it was very soft and becoming, and designed by Molyneux. I liked it almost the best of my gowns because it was so simple.

I had a black velvet wrap to go with it and I wore no jewellery because I hadn't got any.

When I looked at myself in the mirror, I thought perhaps I had made a mistake and should have worn something more elaborate. I would have changed everything at the last moment if I hadn't been afraid of keeping David waiting.

I went down to the Hall and the moment I saw his Bentley draw up outside I ran down the steps.

He didn't seem surprised that I had been waiting for him, he just opened the door and said in his deep voice:

"Good-evening, Samantha!"

It sounded quite different to the way anyone else said it.

I got in. He picked up my hand and kissed it, and I felt a little ripple of excitement go through me.

"You're absurdly lovely!" he said, and now there was a funny, mocking tone in his voice, as if he laughed at himself and me.

He started up the car and we drove off.

I hadn't asked where we were going. It was just so wonderful to be beside him and I knew that was what I had been longing for all day. So much so that I could hardly believe now that he was really there.

One thing I had done during the luncheon break was to buy a copy of his book.

There was a huge pile of them in Hatchards and while I was buying my copy, three others were sold to people picking them up off the counter. I was glad for David's sake that they were selling so well.

We had been so busy all day that I had not had a chance to read any of the book, but I looked at his photograph on the back and realised it didn't do him justice.

It was in fact only a snapshot taken against what appeared to be a battlefield.

I read the publisher's comments which said:

"This is undoubtedly the most provocative and disturbing novel which has been written in the post-war years. David Durham expresses all the frustrations and the anger of the younger generation against the muddled thinking, the inept attitude of politicians and the grave social injustices that are being callously perpetrated on every side.

Never has there been a stronger or more violent clarion call from the youth of this generation for a rebellion against the *laissez-faire* existing in England today."

"You're not going to read that book, are you?" Melanie asked as I turned the pages while I was waiting for Giles to photograph me.

"Why not?" I asked.

"You won't understand it," Melanie answered. "Everyone has a different opinion about it. I agree with Lord Rowden who said when I was with him at Ascot that he was fed-up with people who complained. There is a lot of enjoyment to be found in life if one looks in the right places."

I wondered what Lord Rowden considered the 'right places'. I only knew that if David was complaining he would be quite sure of his facts.

I didn't understand a great deal of what he had said to me last night. But he had a positive way of speaking which made everything he said seem utterly and completely convincing.

He hadn't been talking about his book, *Vultures Pick Their Bones*, but about another book he was starting to write.

As far as I could make out, there were things going on beneath the surface in every country which every right-minded person would want exposed.

"Won't they hate you for bringing into the open all the things they want to keep hidden?" I asked him.

"Under the circumstances I like being hated," he had replied.

We were driving now, I realised, not towards the West End, where I had expected him to take me, but out of London.

As if he knew I was surprised, and without my saying anything he explained:

"I'm taking you to a quiet little place which I think you will enjoy. It's very difficult to find good food in London these days. This is run by a Frenchman who after being a waiter started out on his own, and everybody who eats there once goes again, so he is making a success of it."

I was quite content to go anywhere with David . . . to the moon if he asked me. I looked at him from under my eyelashes as he drove the car and thought how wildly attractive he was, and yet quite unlike any man I had ever seen before.

"Have you been looking forward to seeing me again?" he asked suddenly, as we drove through the suburbs.

"To-day seemed very long," I answered truthfully.

He gave a little laugh.

"I have been wondering what your hair is like, Samantha, and now I know."

"Do you like it?" I asked.

"Do you really want me to tell you how much?" he enquired.

"Yes, please," I replied and he laughed again.

"You are very clever," he said after a moment, "in managing simultaneously to look one thing and seem another."

"What do you mean by that?" I asked.

"I'm referring to the Samantha poise of looking as if all the erotic secrets of the world lay behind your eyes and being able to speak at the same time with the enthusiasm of a very young girl."

I didn't know what to reply to this because I know only too well now what he meant.

How could he possibly know that Samantha from Little Poolbrook hadn't the slightest idea what was implied by the word 'erotic' and that she sounded eager and enthusiastic because everything was so new and unexpected to her?

I took refuge in silence, and then, a little while later, we drew up at a small pub.

It looked very old, almost like one of the highway inns which still exist in some of the villages near us at home.

David parked the car at the side and we went in through a small door into a tiny oak-beamed room with a bar which seemed to fill it almost completely.

There were one or two local people drinking beer and we passed through the bar into a room on the other side of it which had a bow-window looking out on to the small garden.

The Proprietor appeared and was delighted to see David. He had reserved us a table in the bow-window. The room was half panelled with very old oak and there were rafters overhead which David told me later were made from ships' timbers.

"It is very nice to see you, *Monsieur* Durham," said the Proprietor, whose name was Henri. "I'm very grateful to you for the people you have sent me."

"Are you doing well?" David asked.

"Very well, and better than I expected, thanks to you."

"In which case I shall expect a superlative dinner this evening," David said. "I have brought you the most beautiful lady in London to enjoy it."

"*Enchanté, Mademoiselle*," Henri said.

Then he and David went into a long consultation over the menu.

I didn't mind what we ate. I was just happy to be with David and I felt that he had brought me to this small place because he wanted to be alone with me and not just to show me off as so many other men wanted to do when they took me out.

At last the meal was ordered and David said:

"What would you like to drink, Samantha? I have a feeling you don't enjoy champagne as much as you might be expected to do."

"I don't really like it at all," I answered.

"You're full of surprises," David said. "We'll have a very light white wine, which I'm sure you'll prefer."

He ordered it and when Henri said: "An aperitif, *Monsieur*?" David looked at me again.

"Must I have anything?" I asked. "I really dislike cocktails."

I thought David looked at me rather searchingly as if he hardly believed what I said. But he ordered a martini for himself and a tomato juice for me.

When Henri had gone he sat back and said:

"Are you happy, Samantha?"

"Very, very happy," I answered. "I wanted so much to see you this evening."

Only when I had said it did I think that I had been too

69

gushing, and maybe too truthful. Perhaps David would think I was rushing after him if I appeared too eager.

I turned my head away, but I knew he was looking at me and after a moment he said:

"There's something I want to ask you, Samantha. How many men have kissed you?"

It was not a question I had expected and I felt the colour rise in my cheeks.

For the first time I thought how fast it had been for me to allow him to kiss me when we really knew nothing about each other and he'd not even said that he was attracted to me.

I had told myself that I would never let a man kiss me until I knew that he was really in love with me.

I felt that was what Daddy meant when he said that I must 'keep myself' for the man who would matter in my life.

As far as I was concerned, David was the only person who had mattered, but, of course, I realised it had happened too quickly, and I might not matter at all to him.

So I felt ashamed and my cheeks got redder and redder because I really didn't know what to say.

"You're blushing, Samantha," David said after a moment, in a surprised voice.

Then, as I continued to look away from him across the room, he put out his hand and taking my chin in his fingers he turned my face round to his.

"Why should that question embarrass you?" he asked. "Who has kissed you so that you blush to think about it?"

He spoke quite fiercely, and almost as if he compelled me to tell the truth I said:

"No-one."

"What do you mean – no-one?" he asked roughly.

"I ... I mean ... no-one has kissed me ... except you.'

He took his fingers from my chin and stared at me.

"You expect me to believe that?"

"Why shouldn't you?" I asked.

"Because I don't believe it's possible!"

"Why not?"

"Not looking as you look and being one of Giles Bariatinsky's models."

"What has that got to do with it?" I asked.

It was rather difficult to talk sensibly because David was looking down at me and it seemed to me as if his eyes were penetrating and at the same time suspicious.

I couldn't understand why he should think I was lying to him and yet I felt he did.

I looked away from him again with my eye-lids half shut because I was shy. I suppose it appeared to be my enigmatic look. Anyway just as David was going to say something the waiter arrived with his cocktail and my tomato juice.

It seemed to break some spell that David had cast over me, and then the waiters started hovering around the table, the food arrived and we talked of other things.

At first they were rather trivial and then he began to speak seriously about what he thought and what he felt. I found it absorbingly interesting.

I really knew very little of what was happening outside Little Poolbrook. Daddy took *The Morning Post* but I never seemed to have time to read it.

Anyway I found it rather dull, so that I didn't know about the terrible unemployment there was in the North; the injustice of not being able to take a holiday unless they went without pay; strikes where because their families were on the verge of starvation workmen had to give in however just their cause might be.

David talked of all these things and I realised these were the sort of subjects which he had written about in his book.

"We're not the only country in which these things are

happening," he said. "The greed for money supplants everything else: statesmen and politicians are the same whether they are in America, England or Timbuctoo."

"I bought your book to-day," I told him, "but I haven't had time to read it."

"I hope you will like it," he said. "I wrote it in the form of a novel simply because I knew that an official report or white paper is read by only a handful of people. Novels reach a far larger audience."

He paused to add:

"There is also the chance that it may be made into a film."

"That would be wonderful!" I cried. "I do hope it is."

We had finished dinner by this time and only had two cups of coffee in front of us.

I refused a liqueur but David ordered a brandy.

"May I smoke?" he asked. "You don't, do you?"

I shook my head.

"You don't smoke, you don't really like drink, and you say you have never been kissed until last night," he said mockingly. "You are very unpredictable, Samantha."

I didn't answer and after a moment he said:

"You also blush. I thought that was a forgotten art where young women are concerned."

"I can't help it," I said unhappily.

"I'm glad you can't," he answered. "It's very becoming."

He said it in such a strange way that I replied:

"You make it sound as if I do it on purpose."

"I suppose that would be impossible," he said grudgingly, "but everything about you is contradictory."

"I can't help it," I said again.

"I don't want you to help it," he answered, "but it's upsetting – for me at any rate."

"Why?" I asked in surprise.

"Because," he answered slowly as if he was choosing his words, "when I took you out last night I thought it would be rather amusing, or rather, shall I say, I thought you would amuse me."

"And I . . . didn't?" I asked.

"Not in the way I expected."

Again there was a pause and I said:

"Were you very . . . disappointed?"

He smiled at that.

"No, of course not! I was captivated and entranced in a manner I least expected. This morning I thought I must have been mistaken, but I wasn't."

There was something in his voice which made it hard for me to breathe. There was that faint choking feeling again in my throat but I managed to say:

"I . . . I don't think I . . . quite understand."

"Perhaps there's nothing to understand," he said. "I don't know."

He spoke quite sharply, and I felt as if he had suddenly thrown a bucket of cold water over me.

I don't know why, but it was as if I had said or done something wrong and I didn't know what it was.

David had been talking so animatedly, but now he sat silent just looking at me.

After a moment I said uneasily:

"What's . . . wrong? You make me feel . . . uncomfortable."

"There's nothing wrong," he said. "But if you are really so inexperienced it's puzzling and upsetting."

"Why?" I asked. "What were you expecting me to be like?"

He smiled at that.

"I don't believe you'd understand even if I told you."

"And you don't . . . like me as I am?"

"I like you very much as you are," he answered, "too much, perhaps."

"Can one like someone too much?" I enquired.

"I'm not sure," he replied.

I had a feeling we were saying much more to each other than we were putting into words and yet somehow it was like being in a maze and not knowing the way out.

I felt bewildered and yet at the same time conscious of how wonderful it was to be beside David; to be near him; to be talking to him.

He said he liked me very much. That was something, but I told myself I must be very careful not to let him know how much I loved him.

"A woman must never make advances to a man." I felt sure I had read that somewhere.

But after all, I told myself, I didn't make the first advance. David had kissed me and I had not expected him to do so.

Henri brought the bill, then bowed us out with many expressions of gratitude and the hope that we would come again soon.

I looked up into the sky. It was getting dark. The stars were coming out although there was still a faint glow from the sunset left in the sky.

"It's a lovely, warm evening," I said and realised we were both standing beside the car and David was looking at me.

"Does that mean that you want to go for a drive in the country?" he asked.

"I hadn't thought of it," I answered, "but it would be lovely."

"To-day is Thursday," he said unexpectedly, "to-morrow is Friday. I've a suggestion to make to you. Get in."

He opened the door of the car for me, then walked round and got in beside me. But he didn't start up the engine.

He sat for a moment looking at me then he put his arms round me and kissed me.

It had been wonderful last night, but it was even more wonderful to-night. I felt the same marvellous feeling rising inside me; the same ecstasy seeping over me until it was difficult to think and I could only feel.

It was as if David carried me up to the stars and we were lost in the sky and there was nothing left of the world but ourselves.

It was so wonderful, so magical that when he set me free I could only lie with my head against his shoulder for a moment. Then I turned my face to hide it against his neck.

"Darling!" he said. "Darling!"

"I love ... you!" I whispered. "I ... love you!"

He drew me a little closer. Then he said:

"Do you mean that, Samantha?"

"I mean it!" I answered, "and it's so wonderful ... so unbelievably ... exciting!"

I lifted my face up to his and he was kissing me again.

They were hard, possessive kisses which seemed to draw my heart from between my lips and make it his.

I was his!

I felt that I belonged to him and I knew there could never, never again be another man who could ever mean anything in my life.

After a long time when David had kissed me again and again until I knew that I had reached the very zenith of perfect bliss, his hands touched my hair.

"I still can't believe this is happening," he said. "Do you really swear to me, before God, Samantha, that you have never kissed anyone else before?"

"No-one!" I answered. "Oh, David, it's very different from what I thought it would be like."

"What did you expect?" he asked.

"I don't know," I answered, "but I didn't expect to feel that I ... belonged to you, that I was ... part of you, as I do ... now."

"My darling!" he said.

Then he was kissing me again until I could no longer think

or speak – I could only feel my body vibrating to his.

How long we sat outside the little pub, I don't know.

The only light came from the windows. Later on they went out and we were completely in the dark except for the stars overhead.

"I must take you back, Samantha," David said, and his voice sounded low and husky.

"Must . . . I leave . . . you?" I asked foolishly.

"Not for long, my precious," he answered. "To-morrow is Friday as I told you. I'll arrange something – just leave it to me."

He kissed me again. Then he drove back to London very quickly, although my head was on his shoulder and he had one arm round me.

When we reached the Boarding House I said:

"I don't want to go . . . in. I feel as if we shall lose . . . something . . . something wonderful and precious we . . . found to-night."

"We won't do that," David answered, "I promise you."

He kissed me very gently; first my mouth, then both my eyes, the tip of my nose and then my mouth again.

"Good-night, my little love!" he said. "Go to bed and dream of me."

"How could I dream of anyone else?" I asked.

"I should be very jealous if you did," he replied, and now the laughter was back in his voice.

"When shall I see you again?" I asked.

"What time can you get away from the Studio?"

I thought for a moment.

"Usually early on a Friday," I answered. "So with any luck I should be back here by about a quarter past five."

"I'll pick you up at half past," he said. "Pack some things for the country."

"For the country?" I repeated. "That will be exciting! It will be lovely to get out of London."

"It'll be lovely anywhere with you," he answered.

He kissed me again; a quick, rather hard kiss and then he got out of the Bentley and walked round to help me on to the pavement.

"Good-night, my precious!" he said.

"Good-night, David," I answered.

I wanted to tell him what a perfect, wonderful evening it had been and thank him for my happiness, but there were no words.

Instead I walked up the steps to the Boarding House feeling as if I floated on air, that the whole world was golden, wonderful and indescribably perfect.

When I reached my Bed-room I sat down on the bed and found myself thanking God because I was so grateful for David.

"Suppose," I said to myself, "I had never found him? Suppose I had never known that love was like this? Suppose I had let one of those other stupid young men kiss me?"

I was so lucky – so incredibly lucky to have found love, real love, just as Daddy had hoped I would.

Perhaps it was his prayers, I thought, that had brought David to me. I would write and tell him, and I knew how pleased he would be.

I got into bed and began to plan how we would be married in the little church at home. The flowers would hide the ugliness of it inside, but I knew that any place would seem beautiful if I was marrying David.

I supposed we should have to invite Lady Butterworth and all the people in the village who had known me since I was a child, but they would not really matter.

There would be only one person in the Church as far as I was concerned, and that would be David.

I felt myself thrill at the thought of how he would slip the ring on my finger; how Daddy would say, as I had heard him say a dozen times before:

"Repeat these words after me: 'With this ring I thee wed – with my body I thee worship . . .' "

I would be David's wife.

Burying my face in the pillow I hoped we would not have to wait very long. I wanted him . . . I wanted to be close to him.

I wanted him to love me – to go on loving me – not only in the day-time but at . . . night.

Reflection 12

I was ready by five-thirty the following day only by the skin of my teeth.

There seemed to be such a lot of things to do at the Studio and Giles didn't leave as early as he usually does on a Friday.

I also had a tremendous rush during the lunch-hour because I tore out and bought myself two cotton dresses and a bathing-suit.

I had said to Miss Macey when I arrived in the morning:

"What sort of clothes do I need for the country?"

"What sort of country?" she asked.

"A house-party, I suppose."

"Well, that can mean a lot or a little," she replied.

I thought that Melanie, who was in the changing-room, was not listening, but apparently she was because she came out from behind the curtains to say:

"Who are you going with, Samantha?"

I saw no point in lying so I answered:

"David Durham."

"Ho! Ho!" Melanie exclaimed. "You are getting very grand! Well, I can answer your question. You want everything smart you possess."

My heart sank, but I realised there was some point in what Melanie was saying.

After all David Durham was very smart, and his friends would be those scintillating, polished, elegantly-dressed socialites who really rather frightened me.

I had hoped we might be going to stay with a quiet married couple with no-one else in the house except ourselves.

But when I thought of it, I realised that that was not the sort of party David would like. After all, hadn't I met him a the Meldriths'?

And when he was talking to me he had mentioned all sorts of exciting people with whom he was apparently on familiar terms.

Members of the Government, heads of Industry, broadcasters, newspaper proprietors, they were all just names to me, but I gathered they were interested in David's ideas.

"I'm sure I shall have all the wrong things," I said desperately to Miss Macey, remembering the green muslin I had made myself and how scornful Giles had been of it.

"Don't look so worried, Samantha," Miss Macey replied. "Just take two nice cotton dresses for the day-time, which is all you will want in this heat, and you have plenty of elaborate gowns to wear in the evening."

She had been much kinder to me recently and didn't speak to me in the aggressive tone she used to Melanie and Hortense.

"You'll want a bathing-suit," Melanie said. "I expect you have one."

Of course I didn't possess such a thing, neither had I a simple cotton dress among the clothes Giles had bought for me when I arrived in London.

So I got Miss Macey to write me down the address of a

place where I could buy the dresses and she told me there was a store in Bond Street which sold really attractive bathing-suits.

I felt rather guilty about spending any more money until I had paid back Giles what I owed him. But I wanted to look nice for David, and I felt how terrible it would be for him to be ashamed of me when I was among his grand friends.

The cotton dresses were pretty and really very cheap. The bathing-suit seemed ridiculously expensive considering how little there was of it!

I had to buy a cap as well, which looked rather like the cloche hats that all the fashionable women were wearing on their heads.

I ran back to the studio and arrived only a few seconds before Giles was ready for me. So I had no lunch.

Not that I felt hungry! When I thought about last night I was too thrilled to want to eat and so excited to think that in a few hours I would be with David again.

"Can he really love me as much as I love him?" I asked myself not once but a dozen times during the afternoon.

I remembered the note in his voice when he had said: "Good-night, my little love," and I was sure he did love me, and I was the most fortunate girl in the whole world.

"I must try not to be clinging and tiresome because I am in love," I told myself.

I kept thinking of the whining note there had been in the voice of that woman called Elsie when she had been pleading with Lord Rowden on the roof-garden at the Meldriths' party.

It was so obvious he was bored with her and she was trying to hold on to him when he had no further interest in her.

"It's her own fault," I told myself. "After all, Lord Rowden is a married man and if she let herself get fond of him, she has no-one else to blame!"

I couldn't help feeling a little tremor of fear in case the time came when David got bored with me.

Then I told myself that love ... real love ... grew and increased over the years. It was only the wrong sort that faded and disappeared.

That was why Daddy had been warning me not to get involved with a man unless I was quite sure that he loved me.

Well, I was sure – absolutely sure about David, and I knew that we would be blissfully, marvellously happy together.

I wondered if we would live in the country or in London. I did so hope he would choose the country.

"Am I going to wait for you all day?" Giles asked sharply and I realised I had been dreaming instead of arranging myself in front of the camera.

I tried to concentrate on what he wanted me to do, but all the time I kept thinking of David, seeing his face, hearing his voice, feeling his lips on mine.

It gave me a little thrill every time I thought of it, and when at last Giles left the Studio and I was free to go home I ran down the street into Piccadilly so that I could catch a bus to South Kensington.

I had stupidly forgotten, of course, that the clothes I had accumulated since I had come to London wouldn't go into the suitcase which I had brought with me from the Vicarage, so I had to ask Mrs. Simpson if she could lend me one.

She was rather surprised by my request, but when I explained it was all Mr. Bariatinsky's fault for choosing so many clothes for me, she mellowed and lent me an almost new one.

"I'll be very careful with it," I promised.

"I'm sure you will, Miss Clyde," she replied. "It's what's inside that's important, isn't it? All those lovely dresses which Mr. Bariatinsky photographs you in! I wonder you're not afraid to wear them!"

"I'm always afraid of spoiling them," I confessed.

She smiled and murmured something about my being a lucky young woman, with which I thoroughly agreed, although not for the reasons she meant.

Anyway, with a tremendous scramble I was ready – my suitcases were packed and I had a small round leather hat-box as well.

I went to the hall to ask the porter to collect them from my room, and I saw David's Bentley pull up outside.

I ran down the steps and he got out of the car looking more attractive than I had ever seen him before, in a blazer which had a lot of gold buttons on it. It was, I knew, a Regimental blazer because David had been in the Coldstream Guards.

"How are you, my darling?" he asked.

I felt my heart turn over at the tone of his voice.

"I'm all right," I answered.

"You look lovely!" he said. "Or have I told you that before?"

"It's something I want to hear again," I replied.

His eyes were on my lips and I felt as if he kissed me, and then we just stood looking at each other and somehow there was no need for words.

When the porter came out of the house carrying the two suitcases, they seemed almost too heavy for him. He was only a small man, and he had my hat-box under one arm.

He put them down on the pavement beside the Bentley and David exclaimed:

"Good heavens! What have you brought all that luggage for?"

"You didn't tell me what sort of house-party we were going to," I said, "and I didn't want to bring the wrong things."

"House-party?" he questioned.

"Well, you didn't say if it was a big one or a small one," I went on apologetically. "Sometimes people play tennis or swim, or go to a garden-party unexpectedly and I would hate to have the wrong clothes."

I was talking rather quickly because he had a strange expression on his face. He realised the porter was waiting, and putting his hand in his pocket he gave the man two shillings.

Then David said:

"I didn't say anything last night, Samantha, about a house-party."

"You told me we were going to the country," I said in a puzzled tone.

"That is where we are going," he answered, "somewhere very quiet – just you and I."

I looked at him and I suppose he must have seen that I didn't understand because he went on:

"It's a cosy little inn, rather like the one we went to last night, hidden away in the Chiltern Hills. We will just be together, Samantha."

"With . . . no-one . . . else . . . there?"

"I hope not," he answered, "but if there are, we need have nothing to do with them."

"But . . . I can't . . ."

I stopped. I found it hard to go on with the sentence and David asked:

"You can't what?"

"Go away with you . . . alone," I said, and the words came out in a rush, "without a . . . chaperon, without there being a . . . married woman in the party."

He stared at me for a long moment before he asked:

"Are you serious?"

"When you said we could go to the country," I answered, "I thought we would be staying with . . . your friends."

"You told me you wanted to be with me, and I want to be with you," David said. "Surely that's all that is necessary?"

He seemed to be waiting for my answer and then I said slowly:

"I think it . . . would be . . . wrong."

"What do you mean – wrong?"

I was finding it difficult to answer and then I said almost in a whisper:

"If you . . . made . . . love to me like . . . that, it would be . . . a sin!"

"Good God!" David ejaculated so forcefully that he made me jump. "You can't be serious in saying this to me, Samantha! Where on earth have you come from?"

"From a . . . Vicarage," I answered miserably.

He stared at me in astonishment.

"A Vicarage?" he repeated. "I don't believe it!"

"It happens to be true," I said, "and I think now that what you are suggesting is one of the . . . temptations Daddy said I might find in London."

David put his hand up to his forehead.

"Can I really be listening to this, or am I dreaming?" he asked. "You can't look as you do, Samantha, and talk about sin and temptation just because I ask you to go to the country with me."

"Well, I know it isn't right for us to go . . . alone," I said. "We ought to have somebody with us!"

"And do you think that would make any difference?" he asked roughly. "Who do you suggest we take – the porter? One of the people passing by in the street? Good Lord, Samantha, you are talking like some Victorian Miss of half a century ago!"

He spoke scornfully and I felt afraid because I knew he was getting angry.

He bent down and picked up one of my suitcases.

"We can't stand here talking this nonsense," he said. "I love you, Samantha, and you love me. It's really quite ridiculous to start evoking the Ten Commandments and trying to change all our plans at the last moment."

He dumped my suitcase in the boot of the car and went on:

"If you're worried as to what people will think, which I imagine is your main objection, you can register under a false name or as my wife. I've only ordered one room anyway."

What he said and the way he said it made me feel as if I was frozen to the pavement.

I knew that he despised me for being so stupid. I knew, too, that he was angry because I was making a scene.

But I remember how I had promised Daddy that I wouldn't do anything of which he and Mummy wouldn't approve, and I knew without any argument they would not approve of my going away with David alone to stay as his wife in some country inn.

"I'm sorry if I'm spoiling your week-end, David," I said, "but I can't go with you."

He was just going to pick up the second suitcase as I spoke. Instead he straightened himself to say:

"Don't be a little fool, Samantha. We'll talk about this on our way there."

"I'm not going."

I saw the anger in his eyes but before he could speak a voice said:

"So this is where you've been hiding yourself, Samantha. I've had great difficulty in finding you."

I turned and standing beside me was Lord Rowden.

David and I had been so busy arguing with each other that we hadn't noticed his large grey Rolls Royce drive up and park behind the Bentley.

Lord Rowden was dressed in the same way as David and it

was obvious that he was going to the country.

"I was just going to leave this for you, Samantha. It's an invitation for you to come to lunch on Sunday at my house on the river. I thought it might amuse you and I was very anxious to see you again."

I took the note but for a moment I could find nothing to say. Then Lord Rowden looked at David and said:

"How are you, Durham? I've been hoping you would dine with me one evening."

"Thank you," David said, in a not very gracious tone.

"Perhaps my invitation is too late," Lord Rowden went on to me. "I gather you and David Durham are already going to the country. What a pity! I wish you were coming to stay with me."

"I'm sure Samantha would be delighted to accept your invitation," David said in a hard, bitter voice. "She likes large house parties, and I'm certain you will have a crowd of people staying with you."

"I have indeed," Lord Rowden said quickly. "And I should be overjoyed for Samantha to be my guest, and you too, Durham, if you have nothing better to do."

He paused for a moment and then as if he took in the whole situation he said:

"I'm going to Maidenhead now. Why don't you two follow me? You'll find a lot of friends at Bray Park and the weather is going to be perfect for the river."

"What fun!" David exclaimed. "It sounds exactly what we should both enjoy!"

I heard the note of bitter sarcasm in his voice and I realised that he was arranging this to punish me and there was nothing I could do about it.

I just felt weak and helpless, and although I longed to refuse Lord Rowden's invitation, the words wouldn't come to my lips.

"Then that's agreed," Lord Rowden said quickly as if he

was afraid we would change our minds. "I'll go ahead and see that everything is ready for your arrival."

He looked at David.

"You know where the house is, Durham? I've rented Lord Bray's place for the summer."

"I know it well," David replied.

"Then I'll see you both later," Lord Rowden said. "I'm looking forward more than I can tell you to having you as my guest, Samantha."

He put his hand on my arm for a moment, and then he walked away and got into his Rolls Royce.

I stood staring at David.

"Why did you do that?" I asked.

"That's what you wanted, isn't it?" he said savagely. "Gay, gay people; tinkling laughter; champagne; dancing on the lawn, and of course, plenty of young men to try to kiss you in the bushes. That's so much more respectable than going away with me."

His words hurt me like blows and vaguely I thought I ought to refuse to go anywhere with him or anyone else.

Yet I couldn't find the right words, and when he opened the door of the Bentley I got in and he slammed it shut.

He drove off and I felt so miserable that I didn't know what to say or do.

We drove in silence for a long time and then at last, when I could bear it no longer, I said unhappily:

"I'm sorry, David . . . please . . . I'm sorry."

"I can't quite gather what sort of game you're playing," he said.

"Game?" I questioned.

"Well, looking like you do for one thing; being a Giles Bariatinsky model; and then suddenly going all holy on me! I was quite certain you understood what I suggested last night. What's the idea?"

"It's just that I know it's . . . wrong," I said defensively.

He didn't seem to understand and I added:

"People I know don't do that sort of thing unless they are married."

David gave a kind of shout.

"Married?" he said. "So that's the key to the puzzle, is it? You are holding out for marriage, Samantha?"

There was a silence and then I said in a very small voice:

"Do you ... mean you ... don't want to ... marry me?"

David didn't answer for a moment and then he slowed the car down and drove off the road in the shadow of some trees.

He switched off the engine and turned half round in his seat to face me.

"I think we ought to get this clear, Samantha," he said.

I looked at him apprehensively as he went on:

"We seem to be talking at cross-purposes. Last night was an enchantment I shan't easily forget. I find you very, very attractive. You told me you loved me, but I'm not the marrying sort."

I felt as though my heart dropped six feet with a bang, and I felt too that all the lovely plans I had made last night were like a castle of cards which David had knocked down with a touch of his hand.

"I quite understand you want to get married," he went on as I didn't speak. "I suppose all women want that and I'll be frank with you and say that quite a lot of women have wanted to marry me. But you are going the wrong way about it, Samantha."

"What have I ... done that is ... wrong?" I asked.

"Looking like you do and taking up your particular career," he answered, "is not the best introduction to St. Margaret's, Westminster."

I knew that was the fashionable Church where all the

Social brides got married, but I had been thinking of the Church at home and Daddy marrying me to David.

David's eyes were on my face, and now he said in a more gentle voice:

"You are very lovely, Samantha, and I think we could be very happy together, if you would forget your absurd ideas about sin and all that sort of thing."

"I can't help . . . knowing what is . . . right and what is . . . wrong," I said.

"What you think is right for you is not right for me," David answered. "Perhaps I should have made it clear from the very beginning that I have no wish to marry anyone."

"Then if we are not married, we can't possibly stay away together, pretending that we are."

He had made his position clear and I felt I had to make mine clear too.

"Tell me why?" David asked.

"Because it would be . . . wicked."

"But if we were clever no-one would know or have the least suspicion, so why should it matter?"

I wanted to say that God would know, but I felt he might laugh at me and so I merely said nothing and after a moment David said very beguilingly:

"Let's forget this silly argument, Samantha. Let me take you to this little inn. I won't do anything you don't want me to do, not until we have talked it over. I have a feeling, Samantha, that you would realise how very wonderful it would be for us to be alone with each other and know that nothing else is of any importance."

He put his arm around me as he spoke and drew me close to him.

I felt myself quiver because he was touching me. Then he turned my face up to his and I knew he was going to kiss me.

I wanted that kiss more than anything I have ever wanted

in my life before, but at the same time, I realised he was tempting me.

This was just like the temptations I had read about in the Bible, and I knew I had to say no.

With what was really a superhuman effort I turned my face away from David and said:

"We can't ... we mustn't ... I know it's wrong!"

"Damn you!" David said sharply. "You would try the patience of a saint!"

He took his arm away from me, switched on the engine, slammed in the gears and drove off.

I knew he was angry but there was nothing I could do about it.

It would have been so easy, so very easy, to agree with what he suggested, and so very difficult to go on being obstinate. But, I told myself, I could never face Daddy again if we stayed in that inn, and in only one room.

We drove in silence to Maidenhead and then took a twisting, winding road along the side of the river until we came to an enormous house surrounded by elaborate gardens which sloped down to the river's edge.

We drove up to the front door and several footmen came hurrying out to take our cases.

A chauffeur appeared and drove away the Bentley, and David and I walked into the Hall which was very impressive.

A Butler led us across it and opened the door into a long room which seemed to be filled with people, all chattering at the tops of their voices.

For a moment I could see no-one I knew and then Lord Rowden came towards us from one of the windows which opened out on to the lawn.

"I thought you wouldn't be very far behind me," he said. "Need I tell you, Samantha, how pleased I am to see you?"

He took my hand and raised it to his lips and I felt a shiver when his mouth touched my skin.

I wished I had kept on my gloves.

He took me by the arm and introduced me to his guests.

The women were all very pretty. Some of them had titles; some, I gathered, were actresses and some were beautiful – those Lord Rowden introduced just by their Christian names.

There was nobody I had ever met before, although some of the men were very distinguished and I had seen photographs of them in *The Tatler* and other magazines.

David seemed to know everybody and I noticed that one woman who was introduced to me as Lady Bettine Leyton simply flung herself at him.

"David, darling!" she cried. "I had no idea that you were to be here. What a wonderful surprise!"

She put both her arms round his neck and kissed him.

"I'm furious with you," I heard her say in a low voice, "because you haven't been to see me. I had so much I wanted to tell you."

"You can tell me now," David suggested.

"I will and make no mistake about it," she replied.

He laughed at that and I could see he was at his ease and obviously rather pleased with everyone fawning on him, while I felt stiff and there was a large piece of ice somewhere inside me because David and I had quarrelled.

Champagne and cocktails were being handed round on silver trays by the footmen, and Lord Rowden put a glass of champagne in my hand and drew me outside into the garden.

"I want you to see how attractive this place is," he said.

"It's lovely!" I answered, looking at a profusion of roses of every colour.

"I thought I had lost you, Samantha," Lord Rowden said in a low voice. "I had great difficulty in gouging your address out of that snooty secretary of Bariatinsky's."

I felt rather guilty about poor Miss Macey getting the blame for my determination not to see Lord Rowden again.

"But never mind, you are here now," he went on. "I want you to enjoy yourself and now I'll have the chance to tell you all the things I had stored up to talk to you about, if you had dined with me when you promised you would."

"I promised to let you know if I could," I corrected, "and I did telephone."

"You didn't talk to me," he said with a smile as if he knew I had deliberately given a message to his secretary.

"Do you have boats on the river?" I asked to change the subject.

"I'll take you out in my motor-boat to-morrow," Lord Rowden replied. "There's not time now before dinner."

"No, of course not," I said quickly.

"You are very beautiful, Samantha!" he said. "Far too beautiful to be wasted on tiresome young men. I want to wrap you in chinchilla, cover you with diamonds and spend my life telling you how much you excite me."

There was a note in his voice which frightened me and I turned away from him and walked back into the Drawing-room.

I looked for David but he wasn't in the room, nor was Lady Bettine.

Lord Rowden had followed me.

"Are you running away from me, Samantha?" he asked, with an amused note in his voice.

"I would like to go upstairs and rest before dinner," I said.

"Yes, of course," he answered. "Let me show you your room. It's one of the nicest in the house."

I walked towards the Hall and he followed me.

"There's no need for you to come upstairs," I said. "You should be with your guests."

"Are you telling me how I should behave in my own house?" he asked.

"No, no, of course not," I said quickly. "I . . . I just didn't wish to be a . . . nuisance."

"You could never be that," he answered.

We went up the big, broad staircase side by side and moved across the wide landing. He opened a door and I saw what I realised at once must be one of the best rooms in the house.

It was very large and had a huge canopied bed draped with turquoise blue silk, caught up at the sides with gold angels.

There was a long French window opening on to a balcony with windows on either side of it and the furniture was all inlaid and obviously very valuable.

There were two maids unpacking my suitcases and hanging my dresses up in the wardrobe.

"I think you will be comfortable here," Lord Rowden said, "and if you want anything you only have to ask."

"Thank you," I said, "thank you very much."

He looked at me with his dissolute eyes and I felt there was a meaning in them that I didn't understand. I was glad when he went away, shutting the door behind him.

"Your bath's ready, Miss," one of the maids said, and I started to undress.

I suppose if I hadn't been so worried and unhappy about David I would have been curious, if not excited, that I was staying in such a grand house.

I realised there must be masses of rooms full of valuable furniture, and the family pictures, which of course were all of Lord Bray's ancestors, were very interesting.

I only wished I knew something about them, but I was as ignorant about art as I was about everything else.

I was glad I had brought my best evening dresses as I realised there would be plenty of competition from the other women in the party.

I chose a dress of green chiffon. The skirt was made of

layer upon layer of petals which shaded from the palest green of the bodice down to quite a deep emerald where the dress almost touched the floor at the back.

There was a long piece of chiffon falling from one shoulder which could be draped across the front, and I knew when I went downstairs that it was unlikely that anyone would have a prettier dress than mine.

Lady Bettine however was not going to let me get away with being too pleased with myself.

"I always loved that dress," she said when I appeared. "I had the same model in a different colour last year – or was it the year before? Anyway, I remember it was quite a success."

I realised that the other women were listening to see what I replied to what was obviously a 'catty' remark, but I merely smiled and said sweetly:

"I'm sure you looked very pretty in it."

David didn't appear until just before dinner was announced, so I didn't get a chance to speak to him. Anyway I had the feeling he was avoiding me.

He was seated a long way from me in the Dining-room with Lady Bettine on one side of him and a very pretty girl with fair hair on the other.

'He's got a choice of a brunette or a blonde,' I thought bitterly and found it difficult to listen to what Lord Rowden was saying to me.

I was on his left, which surprised me because I should have thought there was someone in the party more important than I to claim that particular place.

But he explained that away as soon as dinner started.

"We are very informal here," he said. "I try to put everyone where I think they will be most amused. I know that your friend David will enjoy himself with Bettine."

"Are they old friends?" I asked.

"Shall we say very close friends?" he replied. "But I must

not give Durham's secrets away. He won't thank me for that."

I knew quite well what he was inferring and although I tried not to care I felt a painful stab of jealousy.

Lady Bettine was very attractive. She had dark eyes that slanted up at the corners and a very red mouth which seemed somehow provocative when she talked to a man.

I thought there was a great deal of mystery and allure about her, and it was quite obvious that, if David thought me attractive, he would find her very attractive too.

Lord Rowden was saying all sorts of flattering things, but somehow I couldn't listen to them.

I kept wondering if David was still angry with me and if we would get a chance to 'kiss and make up' before we went to bed.

I had always been brought up to believe that you should never let 'the sun go down on your wrath', and the last thing I wanted now was to go to bed without saying I was sorry, and asking David to forgive me.

I wondered if after what had happened he would stop loving me.

Later there was dancing to the gramophone, but David didn't ask me to dance although he moved slowly round the floor with Lady Bettine clinging to him like a postage-stamp.

I've never seen anyone dance so close with her cheek glued against his, and I felt it was quite unnecessary.

"Come into the garden," Lord Rowden suggested, but I was too sensible for that.

"I'm very tired," I said, "I've had a hard week. If you won't think it rude, I should like to go to bed early."

"But of course," he said. "I will be very kind and considerate to you to-night, Samantha, and then to-morrow, when you feel rested, there are a lot of things I want to talk to you about."

I didn't like the look in his eyes, so I didn't ask the obvious question. I merely said, "Good-night", and slipped away upstairs.

It was only half past eleven but I really was tired.

I locked my door because I remembered Hortense telling me a long story about how someone had walked into her room at a party and given her a fright.

"I suppose it never struck you that you might have locked your door?" Miss Macey had said sarcastically.

"I didn't think it necessary," Hortense answered, and Miss Macey had looked at her scathingly.

I not only locked the door of my Bed-room but I found there was another door from the bathroom which led into the passage and I locked that too. Then I got into bed.

I fell asleep instantly and if anyone did try to disturb me I certainly didn't hear them.

The next day was one of the most horrible days I can ever remember.

The sun was shining. My new dress was very pretty and I hurried downstairs longing to talk to David.

He was playing tennis! He played tennis all the morning!

We had a long-drawn-out lunch with him right at the other end of the table. Then we went on the river in boats. David went with Lady Bettine and I was left with Lord Rowden.

Fortunately, although he tried to arrange for us to be alone, the woman called Elsie had arrived for lunch and she was as determined to be with him as I was determined not to be, so it worked out quite well.

Elsie's name was Lady Gradley, and to my surprise I found she has a husband who is quite a well-known peer.

I had somehow imagined she was a pathetic, love-sick girl who had lost her heart to Lord Rowden.

There was no doubt however, that she was in love with

him, and she kept trying to attract his attention, take his arm and flirt with him. But he was quite obviously bored with her.

Apparently she had come to lunch with some people who lived nearby and he hadn't known she was one of the party until they actually arrived.

I must say I wouldn't lower myself to behave like that, however fond I was of a man.

I had thought it would be great fun to go up the river and look at all the people bathing and boating, but I kept thinking about David and hoping he was missing me as much as I was missing him.

I wondered what he was talking about to Lady Bettine and if perhaps he was kissing her.

The idea made me feel so unhappy that when we got back to the landing-stage at the bottom of the garden I jumped out first, and, seeing a girl who was called Sonia lying on the lawn with a young man, I asked:

"Have you seen David Durham?"

"I expect he is playing tennis or in the swimming-pool," Sonia answered.

Lord Rowden, who had hurried up behind me, must have heard the last word.

"Have you seen the swimming-pool, Samantha?" he asked. "Come and look at it. I would like to see you in a bathing-suit."

I made up my mind there and then that unless David was swimming I had no intention of doing so.

When we reached the swimming-pool there was no sign of him. Lord Rowden felt the water.

"It's very warm," he said. "Shall I send for your bathing-suit? I expect you have a pretty one with you."

"Yes, I have one," I answered, "but I don't want to swim."

"I want you to," he insisted.

"It's not as warm as all that," I said quickly. "Being so thin I feel the cold."

"You have a perfect figure," he answered, "and the most entrancing legs."

He spoke in a way which made me feel uncomfortable. I didn't like the way he was looking at me. It was almost as if he saw me without any clothes on.

"I might swim later – I don't know," I said coldly.

I walked away to the house and he made no effort to stop me.

When I got to my Bed-room I sat down at the desk and wrote a letter to Daddy. I owed him one anyway, and it made me feel calmer and less on edge about David just to write to Daddy and tell him to take care of himself.

Then I lay on the bed until dinner time.

Lord Rowden had told me that there was to be a big dinner-party with guests coming in afterwards and we were going to dance not to the gramophone, but to a small Band.

I kept feeling it would be rather fun, if only David was nice to me. But I hadn't spoken to him all day, and there was still that heavy lump of ice inside me because he was angry.

I put on one of my prettiest dresses. I knew that Lady Bettine would say it was last year's model, but it was of white tulle with tiny diamantés sparkling on the skirt like dew-drops, and the bodice was embroidered with them.

I felt perhaps it was rather grand for a party in the country, but the other women were even more elaborately dressed and some of the dresses were cut so low at the back that when the wearer was seated she looked as if she had nothing on at all.

Once again I was next to Lord Rowden. I couldn't seem to get away from him and after dinner he insisted on dancing with me the moment the men joined the ladies in the Drawing-room.

"I was very considerate to you last night, Samantha," he said in my ear, "and now I want you to be a little grateful."

"In what way?" I asked warily.

"I'll tell you that later," he said, "but first I have a present for you. Shall we go and look at it?"

"Ought you not to stay here with your guests?" I asked. People from other house-parties kept arriving, but Lord Rowden didn't stop dancing. He just waved to them.

"I'll talk to them later," he said. "Let me show you what I've bought for you."

He danced me to a door at the far end of the room and with his arm still round me drew me into an ante-room, and through that we entered another room which was small and beautifully decorated in the French style.

Lord Rowden shut the door behind him and I felt we were very alone.

"I'm sure we oughtn't to leave your party like this," I said nervously. "People will think it odd."

"They'll think it quite natural where you are concerned," Lord Rowden said, "and all the other men are wishing they were in my shoes."

He opened the drawer of a table which stood near the fireplace and took out a long leather box.

"I bought this for you, Samantha," he said. "I hope you will like it."

"What is it?" I asked.

I thought perhaps it was a fan as the box looked rather the shape, but when I opened it there was a watch-bracelet inside set with diamonds.

I stared at it in astonishment.

"Let me put it on for you, Samantha," Lord Rowden said with a kind of silky note in his voice.

I shut the box with a little slam.

"It's very kind of you," I said, "but I'm afraid I couldn't

accept such an expensive present from someone I hardly know."

"That's something that can easily be remedied," Lord Rowden answered. "I want to know you, Samantha, I want it very much."

He put out his arms as he spoke and I knew he was going to try to kiss me.

I avoided him rather adroitly and said quickly in a breathless voice:

"It's very ... kind of you ... and thank you very much ... but it's much too ... grand a present."

I put the box down as I spoke on a table beside the sofa, and then before Lord Rowden could realise what I was doing, I ran across the room, opened the door and slipped out.

As I shut the door behind me I heard him call my name. Then I ran across the ante-room and back to where everyone was dancing.

I looked around but there was no sign of David, and then I saw to my relief a young Guardsman who had once taken me out to dinner.

"Hello, Samantha!" he said, and was obviously pleased to see me.

"Will you dance with me, Gerry?" I asked.

"Of course," he answered and we were moving quickly to a fox-trot when I saw Lord Rowden come back into the room.

I thought he might look annoyed, but he didn't and I hoped that he had understood that I was not the type of girl who took expensive presents from strangers.

'He must be very rich,' I thought to myself, 'to throw diamonds about like that!'

I thought of him trying to kiss me and realised how stupid it had been to go with him into another room even though he had been very persuasive.

I was determined not to make the same mistake twice.

I danced with Gerry and two friends of his who were in the same house-party and who had all been in the same Regiment.

They talked very like each other about the same things, made the same jokes and paid me the same compliments, so it was rather hard to remember which one I was with.

Lord Rowden didn't ask me to dance with him again, as I had somehow expected he would, and I was thankful about that.

By one o'clock the guests who had come from other houses began to leave, and it was then I thought I had a chance to slip away unnoticed and go to bed.

It had been a horrid day and an even worse evening because David had not once spoken to me nor asked me to dance.

I realised he was very angry with me, and I wondered if I should write him a note to tell him how sorry I was and ask him if we could go back to London early the next day.

If he agreed we could have lunch somewhere and, I thought, talk, so perhaps I could persuade him to see my point of view and not be angry any more.

In my Bed-room I undressed. Then I decided I would write to David and sat down at the desk.

I had put on a pretty blue dressing-gown with lace trimming which Miss Macey had bought for me over my nightgown.

Even so there was a chill little wind blowing in from the river so I got up to close the long French window which opened on to the balcony.

As I did so I looked out and saw it was a moonlit night and the gardens looked very beautiful. The river glimmered like a ribbon of silver. There was something romantic about it which made me feel even more unhappy because David wasn't with me.

I kept thinking how wonderful it would be if David and I could go up the river alone in a punt or a canoe, and he would kiss me under the over-hanging branches of the trees.

We could be very close together, as we had been in the Bentley ...

The idea tortured me so I pulled down the blind over the French window.

I didn't pull the curtains as the maids had done over the other two windows of my room, but just the blind, so that I wouldn't see the moonlight outside while I was writing my letter to David.

I began ... I wrote about three lines ... then I tore it up. I tried again. It was hard to know what to say.

How could I write what was really a love-letter to some-body who was angry with me and perhaps didn't love me any more?

It seemed hopeless. I made half a dozen attempts and they all ended up in the waste-paper basket.

I sat thinking of what I should say next, and then quite unexpectedly I heard a very soft knock on the door of my room.

For a moment I thought it might be David, then I knew that David would never knock like that.

I don't know why, but I felt he would never do anything sort of stealthily and surreptitiously, and this knock was both.

I switched out the lamp on the desk and listened. As there was no light, whoever it was outside might think I was asleep.

The moonlight shining through the blind over the window was strong enough for me to see that now somebody was turning the handle of the door.

I could see the knob twisting, but as it was locked, the door wouldn't open.

Then I heard a whisper.

"Samantha! Samantha!"

I knew who it was. I knew that silky, over-confident voice only too well, even though he was whispering.

"He'll think I'm asleep," I told myself.

I was glad I had had the sense to lock not only the Bedroom door, but also the one out of the bathroom.

I thought I heard footsteps going down the passage but I wasn't certain because the carpet was very thick, and yet I was sure he had gone away.

I gave a sigh of relief.

It was rather frightening and eerie to hear those knocks and my name whispered on the other side of the door. I got up from the writing-table and walked towards the bed.

I was just beginning to undo the sash of my dressing-gown when I heard a sound, just a tiny scrape, as if someone moved a chair. It came from outside on the balcony.

I held my breath and then I saw against the blind a huge dark shadow.

I don't know why but the shadow was more frightening than if I had seen Lord Rowden himself.

It was like all the goblins that had frightened me as a child rolled into one.

I remembered then that I had not locked the window. I had merely pulled it to. I was terrified and it made me run across the room and unlock the door into the passage.

The landing and stairs were in darkness, but the windows in the Hall were un-curtained and the moonlight was streaming in.

I flew down the stairs and knew with some detached part of my mind that the front door would be heavily bolted and barred. So I rushed down a passage which led to a door at the side of the house which opened on to the swimming-pool.

I had come in that way in the afternoon when I had said I

would fetch my bathing-suit. I reached the door, found it was locked, but the key was in the lock and there was only one bolt at the bottom.

I opened it and still driven by a wild fear which I couldn't explain even to myself, I started running away from the house in the direction of where I thought stables would be.

I passed the swimming-pool and was moving over the grass with a high yew-hedge on one side of me when I ran into a man.

I gave a scream of terror and then as his arms went round me I realised it was David.

"Samantha!" he said sharply. "What's the matter?"

"Oh ... David ... David!" I said, my voice almost incoherent because I was so breathless, "take me away ... please ... take me away ... I can't stay here ... I can't!"

"What's happened? What's the matter?" he asked again.

I held on to him, finding it very hard to get my breath, terrified that he would leave me.

"Take me away!" I cried again. "He's trying to get into my Bed-room from the balcony."

"Who is?" David asked then added before I could speak, "Need I ask? I should have known that swine would try something like this."

He held me very close and I felt secure and safe and no longer so afraid, but I was still trembling.

"Where were you going?" he asked.

"I was just trying to get ... away," I answered. "He ... frightened me."

"I'll take you back to London," David said, and added savagely: "We shouldn't have come here in the first place."

I had no answer to that and with his arm round me we walked through the garden until we found the stables where the cars were garaged.

There was nobody about and David got out his Bentley.

"Get in," he said. "But I can't take you to London like that."

For the first time I realised I was only wearing my nightgown and a dressing-gown.

"I ... I can't ... go b-back to my ... room," I said, my voice shaking.

"No, of course you can't," he said. "Don't be frightened, Samantha, everything is all right now."

"You are ... not still ... angry with me?" I asked.

He didn't answer for a moment and then he said:

"I have a feeling that I've behaved rather badly. Do you forgive me, my darling?"

"Of course I do," I said quickly. "It's just that I've been so ... unhappy. Lord Rowden ... frightened me ... and everything has been ... h-hateful!"

My voice broke on the last word.

David put his hand over mine.

"You are cold," he said gently. "I'm going to get you some clothes and then we'll go back to London."

He started up the car without saying any more and drove round to the kitchen-quarters of the house.

He stopped. Then he bent forward and kissed my mouth.

"Don't be frightened, my sweet," he said. "I may take a little time to get your things, but you'll be quite safe here until I come back."

He went away, disappearing into the darkness of the house, and I was no longer afraid. Actually, I don't think I was even cold.

I was happy ... ridiculously, gloriously happy, because David had kissed me again.

Reflection 13

Lady Meldrith looks more like a pretty parakeet than when I last saw her.

She is obviously delighted to see Giles and gushes:

"How sweet of you to come and to bring little Samantha with you."

As I am at least six inches taller than she is I can't help feeling that the 'little' refers more to my station in life than to my actual height.

The Drawing-room, when it isn't full of people, is most impressive and the flowers, all hot-house and very expensive, are beautifully arranged.

I hoped I would see someone I know, but although they are familiar faces from the magazines there is no-one I have actually spoken to before.

Prince Vezelode of Russia is rather disappointing. He is tall and was obviously good-looking when he was young, but he is now over fifty.

"What has the Prince been doing since the Revolution?" I ask the man standing beside me. I never heard his name, but I gather he is a Member of Parliament.

"Washing-up in some sleazy European restaurant, I expect," he answers.

I look surprised, and he says:

"We oughtn't to laugh about it; the Russian aristocracy have had a terrible time in the last eleven years since they escaped from the Bolsheviks."

"The Prince looks very prosperous now," I say.

I notice that he has enormous pearl and diamond studs in his white shirt. My companion smiles.

"He has Wilfrey's Waffles to thank for that."

I wait for the explanation and he adds:

"That's the Princess – the fat little woman with dyed hair talking to our host. She was a Miss Wilfrey and a packet of their famous waffles stands on every American breakfast table."

I laugh and then I say:

"Talking of waffles makes me feel quite hungry. Surely it's time for dinner?"

I am hungry owing to the fact that we worked all through lunch-time with a very special order which Giles had promised to do in record time.

I wish that editors were a little more considerate and would make up their minds what they want before the last moment. We always have a rush just as the paper is 'going to bed' – which seems to me a most inappropriate expression.

My companion is counting.

"We are twenty-nine," he says, "and as I imagine there will be an even number of dinner guests there is obviously one more to come."

Even as he speaks I see someone come in through the door and I know who it is!

My heart seems to leap in the air and turn several somersaults, and I have the uncomfortable feeling that I'm going to faint.

It is David! The one person I was sure I wouldn't see here to-night . . . David!

I want to run away, to hide and I can't think what I can possibly say to him!

Reflection 14

They say that when a person is drowning they see their whole life pass before their eyes in the space of two seconds.

I know that when David walked into the room a few minutes ago that's what happened to me.

Not indeed my whole life, but I saw again everything that had happened that miserable week before he went away.

He was so kind when he drove me back from Bray Park that I felt all our misunderstandings were over.

In some extraordinary way of his own and doubtless by tipping lavishly he got the night-watchman to wake up a housemaid who packed my clothes. The watchman then brought my suitcases and David's to the car.

Before that, David had come back to me and told me what he had arranged. He sat in the car beside me and I slipped my hand into his and said:

"Please . . . forgive me."

"I've told you already," he answered, "that I'm the one who needs forgiveness."

He held my hand very tightly and nothing seemed to matter, not even the fact that I was wearing my dressing-gown, which, I realised, would look rather peculiar when I arrived back at the Boarding House.

But David solved that problem too. We stopped on our way back to London and he opened my suitcase. He found a dress that had a warm jacket and told me to go into the wood by the side of the road and put it on.

He was so sweet and understanding that I didn't feel embarrassed and changed behind a tree in the moonlight. Then

David packed my night-gown and dressing-gown for me and we drove on.

When we arrived at the Boarding House he kissed me gently and said:

"You are tired, Samantha, and you've had enough to put up with to-night. Try not to worry about us . . . or anything else. Just go to sleep."

"When shall I see you?" I asked, knowing I should have waited for him to say that, but the words were out before I could stop them.

"I'll pick you up at eleven o'clock," he answered. "Wear something simple and we'll go and have lunch somewhere in the country."

The next day we drove out of London well away from the direction of Bray Park and found an amusing little Pub, in a small village in the depths of Hertfordshire.

The food wasn't very good, but I didn't mind, and David didn't seem to either, and we talked for hours, about all sorts of things, except, I remembered afterwards, about ourselves and our love.

It was as if we both knew that was a controversial subject and were determined to avoid a quarrel! But of course, it cropped up again that evening after we had been out to dinner and continued to do so every night.

David wanted me to go back to his flat and I wouldn't.

I was afraid that when we got there I would let him make love to me, after which there would be no more need for arguments about whether I should go away with him for the week-end or not.

"Are you afraid of me, Samantha?" he asked, when I refused to do what he wanted.

"I suppose I am," I replied, "but also of . . . myself."

"Can't you understand," he said, "that love is so important that we shouldn't waste it in this ridiculous manner — loving each other, and yet not being happy as men and women have been happy since the beginning of time?"

I didn't answer, but he knew what I was thinking.

"Do you really believe marriage would make us any happier?" he asked savagely. "It's only because, like all women, you want to put a man in a cage. You want to fence him in as if he were a wild animal and keep him all to yourself. I would get claustrophobia, Samantha, and all the weeping in the world wouldn't stop me going away if I wanted to."

"At least I should be your wife," I said unwisely.

"And what difference would that make?" he asked. "Except of course, I should have to support you financially."

"I wasn't thinking of that," I said.

"Well, I am!" he answered. "I not only do not want a wife, but I also can't afford one."

I looked surprised because, after all, he owns a Bentley, and I know, although I haven't been to his flat, that it is a very expensive block and that he has a man-servant to look after him.

As usual David knew what I was thinking.

"I'm making money at the moment," he said. "Of course I am. But how long will it last? People like me have turned out only a 'flash in the pan' before now, and the promise of a film may be just 'pie in the sky' – who knows?"

All that week I seemed to be suspended between Heaven and Hell.

One moment I would be ecstatically, wonderfully happy because David was sweet to me and I knew he loved me. The next moment he would say something bitingly sarcastic, and I would feel utterly despondent and in the depths of misery.

I suppose we were both very much on edge by the time Friday came round, and there was the inevitable question hanging over me as to whether I would go away with him or not.

Sometimes he would try to coax me.

"Be sensible, darling," he would say in that voice which would have charmed a bird out of a tree. "I love you! I've never met anyone so utterly and completely fascinating, and it's only natural that you should excite me. I want you to belong to me. I want you all for myself."

He would kiss me until the world whirled round me and I felt as if we were alone in a Paradise of our own.

Then breathlessly I would have to say:

"No ... David! ... No!" and come down to earth with a bang!

"Damn you!" he said once. "You're enough to drive a man to drink!"

I was just going out to get some lunch on Friday when the telephone rang and as I pulled open the door of the Studio, Miss Macey said:

"It's for you, Samantha."

I ran back hoping it was David, and it was.

"Listen, Samantha," he said. "They're starting the film of my book and I've got to go to America. If I hurry I can get on the *Queen Mary* at Southampton to-night."

"To-night?" I repeated.

"Yes," he replied, "but it's going to be a rush. Could you be very sweet and pack my things for me? I had no idea this was likely to happen and I've given my man the day off."

"Yes, I will pack for you," I said.

"I'll telephone the porter and tell him to let you into the flat," David went on. "You'll find my suitcases in a cupboard in the hall. I'll need tails and a dinner-jacket."

"How long will you be away?" I asked in a very small voice.

"I've no idea," he answered. "They have cast the film, it's definite. Hurry, Samantha, or I shall miss the train from Waterloo."

I jumped into a taxi and went to his flat.

It was the first time I had seen it and thought it very attractive with a big red leather sofa and red curtains to match. There were masses of books, and the furniture, even to my inexperienced eyes, was antique and obviously valuable.

The Bed-room was nice too, if rather severe. I found the suitcases where David said they would be and started to pack his clothes.

Fortunately Mummy had shown me years ago how one should pack for a man with the trousers at the bottom of the case, then the coats, the under-clothes and lastly the shirts on top, so that they wouldn't get crushed.

I thought David's pyjamas were very alluring, all in heavy silk and embroidered on the pocket with his initials.

He had white backless waist-coats for the evening which had been invented by Michael Arlen, and although I had never seen him in his tail-coat, I was sure he would look very elegant in it.

I tried not to think while I was packing for him that he was going away from me and how empty my life would be without him.

I knew I was going to feel ghastly once he had gone, but I told myself I must try to be glad for his sake that his book was going to be made into a film, and that he would make lots and lots of money.

I had filled one suitcase and was just putting his handkerchiefs, collars and ties on the top of the second one when the telephone rang.

I picked it up thinking it might be David, and a woman's voice said:

"Can I speak to Mr. David Durham?"

I thought it would seem strange if anyone guessed who was answering the telephone, so I assumed a cockney accent.

" 'E ain't 'ere yet."

"Will you please give him a message when he arrives?" the voice said. "This is Lady Bettine Leyton speaking. Tell Durham that I am leaving now for Waterloo and that I have made the arrangements about the cabins on the ship. Is that clear?"

"Very clear," I answered and hung up.

I stood staring at the telephone for what must have been a long time.

Then I heard a key turn in the door and a moment later David walked in.

"Are you there, Samantha?" he called as he reached the hall. He came into the Bed-room and said:

"You've done my packing! You are an angel!"

Then he looked at my face and asked sharply:

"What's the matter?"

"Lady Bettine has just telephoned," I answered in a voice which didn't seem to belong to me, "to say that she's leaving now for Waterloo and has arranged the cabins on the ship."

I paused – and then added:

"How nice for you to have her next door, or are you going to use only one cabin?"

I saw David's lips tighten and he said:

"To the pure, all things are impure. So that's the construction you put on her message."

"I'm not a fool," I replied. "You needn't pretend she's not going with you ... or why. I saw the way you behaved with her at Bray Park."

David looked at me and I saw the anger in his eyes.

"Is there any reason," he asked nastily, "why I shouldn't behave in any way I see fit?"

"No, of course not," I answered. "All you want is to go away with a woman and any ... woman will do."

I could hardly believe that I was speaking in such a manner, and yet the words seemed to come to my lips without my really willing them.

I had lost my temper, which after all was not so surprising, considering that I have red hair.

David had never seen me in a temper before and it obviously made him furious.

"You can hardly complain," he said unpleasantly, "that someone else is taking your place, if that's what you are inferring. After all, you have made it very clear that your high-flown principles are far more important to you than my feelings."

He spoke so bitterly that I felt my own anger ebbing away and being replaced by an agony of unhappiness which seemed to hang over me like a black cloud.

"I . . . thought we . . . loved each . . . other," I said in a very low voice.

"Love! What do you know about love?" David snapped. "What you want, Samantha, is marriage, or have you forgotten that? You won't give your love, you will only sell it for a wedding-ring. It's a form of prostitution, although I can't expect you to admit it, and it's certainly blackmail."

"If you think I am trying to blackmail you into marrying me, you are mistaken!" I flared at him.

Now I was angry again.

"You can doll it up with pretty phrases and lots of kisses," David said sarcastically, "but it's still blackmail."

"I loved you! I really loved you," I said. "But you don't love me! All you want is that I should give you my . . . body and then you will be off hunting for another girl with a pretty face who is silly enough to give you her heart."

"If it comes to that," David said, "what else have you got to offer me, but your body?"

He paused and there was the light of battle in his eye which I had seen before; a light which meant he was determined to win the argument – intent on being the conqueror.

We were facing each other defiantly and the sun coming

through the Bed-room window turned my hair into fiery gold.

"You have a pretty face," he said slowly, making every word a knife-thrust. "No-one is arguing about that, but you are abysmally ignorant, ridiculously innocent and in consequence a crashing bore!"

I felt as if every word struck deep into my heart and drew blood.

I stood looking at him as the full meaning of what he had said sank deeper and deeper into my consciousness and seemed to swallow me up.

Then I turned and walked out of the room, across the hall and out of the flat. As I slammed the door behind me, I heard him call my name and started to run.

I didn't wait for the lift. I tore down the stairs and into the street.

There was a taxi passing slowly by and I pulled open the door while it was still moving, jumped inside and gave my address through the communicating window.

I didn't look back to see whether or not David had followed me. I knew he wouldn't be able to if he intended to catch the train to Waterloo.

He had to finish his packing and get his suitcases downstairs.

I sat in the taxi feeling very cold but not in the least like crying. I thought to myself: 'This is how people are when they are dead,' because I was certain something had died inside me.

When I got to the Boarding House I went upstairs and started to pack. I knew all my things wouldn't go into my suitcase, so I got one of the maids-of-all-work to fetch me some big cardboard dress-boxes.

I knew there must be plenty of them stored away somewhere in which the dresses that Giles had bought for me had been delivered.

Finally with one suitcase, four large dress-boxes and a bag containing odds and ends, I set off for Paddington Station.

Luckily Mrs. Simpson was out, so I didn't have to tell her a lot of lies or make excuses about why I was leaving. I just told the girl in the office that I didn't know when I'd be back and they were not to keep my room for me.

Then I went home.

Reflection 15

"I say, are you all right?"

The voice of the Member of Parliament seems to come from a very long distance.

I suppose it is less than a minute since David came into the room and yet I feel he has been there for ages.

"I think I would like a drink," I say weakly.

"Of course," my companion says. "Here, take mine while I try to find a waiter."

He puts a glass into my hand and I've drunk everything it contained without even tasting it.

I have no idea if it was champagne, a cocktail or sherry, but it makes me feel better and now when the Member of Parliament turns to speak to me again I am able to smile at him.

"I expect I'm hungry," I explain. "We do seem to have been waiting a long time for dinner."

"I agree with you," he replies. "I hate people who are late, and I like to have my meals on time. Anyway, as I never know when there will be a Division in the House, I eat when I get the chance!"

He laughs and just as if I hear a stranger doing it, I laugh too.

David is shaking hands with one or two people in the room but he is making no effort to come near me, in fact I am not even certain if he has seen me.

"Dinner is served, My Lady!" the Butler's voice seems to boom across the room, and now, thank goodness, we can go down to dinner.

I wonder if I can slip away when it's over without anybody noticing.

I can't meet David ... I can't talk to him ... I have nothing, absolutely nothing to say to him!

Reflection 16

Here I am in the Bentley again. The car that has meant so much to me in the past that it is almost like coming home, and yet, I am determined not to be anything but cold and distant to David.

I can see his profile out of the corner of my eye and he is just as devastatingly handsome as ever, except that he looks a little thinner.

There is something taut and rather fine-drawn about him which I can't remember noticing before.

He is looking straight ahead and he hasn't said a word to me since he came to my side about half an hour after dinner and said quietly:

"I think it's time we left, Samantha. I'm going to take you home."

It wasn't a question of "May I?", or "Will you?". He just stated a fact.

Before I could find an answer he had taken me across the room and out of the Drawing-room without our even saying good-night to Lady Meldrith.

I wanted to expostulate; I wanted to argue with him; but my voice seemed to have got lost, and I had a constriction in my throat which made it almost impossible to breathe.

We waited in the Hall while one of the footmen fetched my wrap, then we went out into Grosvenor Square. David had parked his Bentley exactly opposite the Meldriths' house.

He opened the door, I got in, and only as he turned the ignition-key did he ask:

"Where are you living now?"

I gave him the address, somewhat surprised that he didn't assume I was still at the Boarding House.

I wondered if he had tried to find me there, and then I told myself there was no reason why he should have been interested.

The Meldriths' dinner took so long, although I didn't taste anything I ate, that it is now quite late and the Bentley is moving very fast through the empty streets.

I have a feeling that David wants to talk to me when we reach my flat, and as I have no intention of allowing him to come in I'll do my usual trick of jumping out very quickly as he puts on the brakes.

Here we are!

I expected David to ask if it was the right Square but he seems to know this part of London and now he is drawing up outside my building.

I have opened the door. I am on the pavement.

"Wait, Samantha!" David's voice is sharp, but I pay no attention.

"Good-night, David!" I say and run up the steps.

Reflection 17

It all happened so quickly that even now, when I am no longer so frightened and can think more clearly, I can hardly remember what occurred.

I had the key of the outside door of the flats ready in my hand. But to my surprise, when I reached the top of the steps hurrying away from David, I found that the outer door was open.

I thought it must have been left like that by the woman upstairs who leaves it unlocked for her young man because she is too lazy to come down and open it for him. He is an actor and therefore keeps most irregular hours.

I went in and, still in a hurry, took out my key to put it in the Yale lock of my own door. Then I realised that was open too.

I pushed it and at that moment everything happened.

A man who seemed to be enormous, dark and menacing, rushed at me from behind the door, hit me twice, then ran past me into the Hall.

Even before he hit me I started to scream, and as I staggered and fell against the wall I screamed and screamed again.

There was the sound of somebody running up the steps very quickly. Then David's arms were round me and I was clinging to him but still screaming, except that my voice was muffled against his shoulder.

"What has happened?" he asked. "Who was that man, Samantha?"

"He . . . hit me! Oh, David . . . he hit . . . me!"

"It's all right," he said soothingly. "He has gone now. It must have been a burglar."

"He . . . hit me!" I said again.

I couldn't believe it had happened. My face was burning from his fist, and the other blow had been on my chest.

"There . . . may be . . . another . . ." I cried in terror, and David reached out his hand for the light.

He switched it on, then said sharply:

"Don't look!"

But I had raised my head for a moment from his shoulder and had seen the room and the utter confusion.

Everything had been emptied on to the floor – the drawers, my books and boxes. Chairs and tables were overturned and ornaments broken.

It was so horrible that I started to cry! David picked me up in his arms and carried me across the Sitting-room and into the Bed-room.

The door was ajar and he laid me down on the bed.

He began to take his arms from me but I held on to him.

"Don't . . . leave me! Don't . . . leave . . . me!"

"I'm not going to leave you," he answered.

"There . . . might be . . . somebody in the . . . bathroom," I said and thought to myself that my voice sounded hysterical.

The bathroom was little more than a cupboard at one side of the room. David opened the door and switched on the light.

There was nobody there, and he came back to say:

"I'm sure there was only one man, Samantha."

"He might . . . come . . . back," I murmured weakly.

"That's very unlikely," he replied, "but I'll tell you what I want you to do. I want you to undress and get into bed. While you are doing that I'll lock my car and the doors."

"You won't go . . . away?" I asked nervously.

"I'll come straight back and make you a warm drink," he said. "Now get into bed, Samantha. I shan't be more than a minute or two."

"Promise . . . you won't . . . leave . . . me?" I asked.

"I promise," he said gravely.

He went out of the Bed-room and shut the door carefully behind him, which I knew was because he didn't want me to see the mess in the Sitting-room. I didn't really care what it was like as long as the burglar didn't come back and hit me again.

I undid my dress very quickly and hung it up in the wardrobe, slipped off my other clothes and put on the first night-gown I could find.

Then I got·into bed to lay shivering and listening. I was still afraid that David might change his mind and leave me.

I heard him shut the Sitting-room door and then there was a sound as if he was turning the chairs the right way up again before he switched off the light and came back into the Bed-room.

"There's no sign of your burglar, and I'm sure, Samantha, he is far more frightened of us than we are of him. After all, if we see him again we can hand him over to the Police."

"I don't . . . want to tell the . . . Police what has . . . happened," I said childishly.

"We shall have to see if you have lost anything valuable," David said gravely.

"I haven't got anything valuable to lose," I answered.

"Then that makes it easy," he said. "Now, is there anywhere where I can make you something warm to drink? Warm and sweet was what my Nanny always prescribed for shock."

"There's a kettle and a gas ring in the bathroom," I said.

He smiled at me, opened the bathroom door and I could hear him rattling cups and saucers.

It is very small, but it really is rather cleverly fitted up as a bathroom-cum-kitchen. There is even a board that one can let down over the bath, presumably if you had a lot of cooking to do, which is very unlikely in my case, because I have never cooked for anyone but myself.

I lay back against the pillows and now because David was with me I didn't feel either so cold or so frightened and I wondered why I had been so afraid when he had walked into the Meldriths' Drawing-room. The burglar was far more frightening than he was.

He put his head round the door.

"Have you got a hot water bottle?" he asked.

"It's on a hook," I answered, "but . . ."

I was going to say that he shouldn't bother to fill it for me, but he had gone again, and I felt too weak to shout.

He brought me a cup of cocoa with lots of milk in it and at least four spoonfuls of sugar.

"Drink it all up," he said in the voice which I always obeyed.

I sat up in bed, took it from him and as I did so he said:

"You've got terribly thin, Samantha. What have you been doing to yourself?"

"I look fatter when I'm dressed," I said defensively.

"I noticed how much weight you have lost the moment I walked into the Meldriths' Drawing-room."

"Were you surprised to see me?" I asked.

"I was relieved," he replied. "I was sick of dining with the Meldriths and having you chuck at the last moment."

I was so astonished that I looked at him open-mouthed. But without waiting for me to answer he went back to the kitchen and filled my hot water bottle.

He brought it to me, turning it upside down to be quite certain it wasn't leaking, then held my cup of cocoa while I put the hot water bottle inside the bed.

"Thank you very much," I said. "Do you mean that you asked Lady Meldrith to invite me the other times when I threw her over at the last moment?"

"I couldn't think of anyone else whose invitation you

would feel compelled to accept," he answered. "Even then to-night she had to invite Giles to make quite certain you would turn up."

"And . . . why did you . . . want to see me?" I asked.

"I wanted to talk to you, Samantha," David said in his deep voice.

I felt my heart give a funny jump, and then it started thumping wildly and I wasn't certain if it was because I was frightened or was happy that he wanted to talk to me.

Then suddenly I gave a cry.

"Oh, David, I've thought of something!"

"What is it?" he asked.

"I must get up and get dressed at once!"

"Why?"

"Because I can't stay here," I answered. "I would be terrified. I'd feel certain the burglar would come back if I was alone. I must go to an Hotel."

I finished the cup of cocoa and put the cup and saucer on the table beside my bed.

"If I dress quickly," I said, "will you take me in your car? It would be difficult for me to get a taxi as late as this."

David didn't answer for a moment and then he said:

"Listen, Samantha, it wouldn't be easy for a woman alone to get into an Hotel at this time of night. They'll just say they're full up."

"I can't help that," I said. "I can't stay here. I can't! I can't!"

My voice rose again, I could feel the pain in my face and in my chest where the burglar had hit me, and I remembered how large and menacing he had seemed.

"I shall . . . never feel . . . safe . . . again," I went on with a little sob.

"I'm going to suggest something," David said, "but I don't want to frighten you more than you are already."

"I know you think it's foolish of me," I said, "but I really am terrified. Supposing I had been here alone when that man broke in?"

"I'm sure he made quite certain that you were out before he did so," David said. "Burglars don't usually leave much to chance, Samantha. But I understand you are frightened and that's why I have a suggestion to make."

"A suggestion?"

"That I should stay here with you to-night," David replied. "To-morrow we will make different arrangements so that you won't be afraid."

I looked at him without speaking and he said very quietly:

"You can trust me, Samantha."

"B-but it will . . . be . . . uncomfortable for you," I stammered.

"I've been uncomfortable before," he said with a smile, "and I can assure you the floor here would be luxury compared to some of the places where I have had to sleep."

"There's no need to sleep on the floor," I said. "There's a chair . . ."

I looked round the room. I had never realised before how tiny my Bed-room was or how much room the bed took up.

David watched me and then he said:

"I could sit in a chair in the Sitting-room, Samantha. But I would be farther away and you know the most sensible thing would be for me to lie on the bed. I swear I won't touch you – and it is a very large bed!"

"It came from the Vicarage."

"I'll treat it with proper respect," David said.

Now there was that note of laughter in his voice which I knew so well.

"If you . . . are quite . . . sure . . ." I said hesitatingly.

"I thought you would see sense, Samantha."

He picked up my cup and saucer and took them into the kitchen. Then he came back into the Bed-room, took off his dinner-jacket and put it over the back of the chair.

He undid his shoes, took them off and stood for a moment looking at me.

I always think there's something very attractive about a man in a white shirt without a coat, and David's evening shirts, as I had seen when I packed them, were made of silk. He wore gold cuff-links with his crest on them.

"Are you quite happy about this Samantha?" he asked. "You wouldn't rather I went into the Sitting-room?"

"No," I said quickly. "I would much rather you were near me and, please, will you lock the door so that no-one can creep in on us when we are asleep?"

"They wouldn't surprise me because I'm a very light sleeper," David replied, but he locked the door and then walked to the other side of the bed.

"I think you'd better get under the eiderdown," I said. "It gets cold at night. After all, it is October."

"That would also be a sensible thing to do," David said in a calm, expressionless voice.

He lay down on the bed and pulled the eiderdown over him, I realised there was a big gap between us.

"Shall I turn out the . . . light?" I asked in a nervous little voice.

"I think you might find it difficult to sleep if you kept it on," David answered.

"Yes, I would," I said, and turned it out.

I lay on my back and found it difficult to breathe.

I could hardly believe that we were lying side by side, and that David was with me again. David, whom I had been so afraid to see that I had been trying to hide from him ever since I came back to London!

In fact, before I returned, I had made Giles promise on his most sacred word of honour that if I went back to the Studio he wouldn't tell David where I was living.

After a moment I said:

"I hear your film is a great success."

"So I am told," David replied.

"You don't sound very excited about it."

"I'm not," he answered. "There's only one thing I've been trying to do these past months."

"What was that?"

"To find you."

I was very still.

"What do you . . . mean?"

"How could you disappear like that? Where the devil did you go to?" David asked. "I nearly went mad trying to find you."

"You . . . wanted to . . . find me?" I said in a very small voice.

My heart had started beating again with heavy thumps like a hammer.

"Of course I wanted to find you," he said. "Do you suppose I didn't realise . . ."

He stopped. There was a pause. Then he said very, very quietly:

"I wanted to find you, Samantha, so that I could ask you to marry me."

For a moment I felt I must have dreamt that he had said it, and then as I didn't answer he went on:

"Will you marry me, Samantha? There are a lot of things we have to say to each other and a lot of explaining to do. But that is the only one which really matters. Please, say yes, Samantha."

I gave a little cry.

"I can't, David! I can't! I want to marry you . . . I've always wanted to . . . but it's . . . impossible! Oh, David . . . why do you . . . ask me . . . now?"

I heard my voice ringing out in the darkness and then there was silence, until David said, in a voice that was slow and almost expressionless:

"Will you tell me why you won't marry me?"

I drew a deep breath.

"It's too soon, that's why I didn't want to ... see you. I wanted to wait until I was ... different ... until I had ... changed myself to what you ... wanted me to be, but at the moment ... it's hopeless ... quite hopeless!"

"I may be very dense," David said, "but I can't quite understand, Samantha, what you are trying to say to me. Perhaps you had better start from the beginning and tell me what happened to you after you left me in the flat. I ran after you but you just vanished."

"I got into a taxi," I said. "I went back to the Boarding House and packed, and then I went home."

"I thought that was where you had gone," David said, "but you see, you never told me where your home was. I knew it was in Worcestershire but that was all."

"I didn't think you would be interested," I said.

"I was sure you would have gone to the Boarding House when they told me you hadn't been back to the Studio."

"How did you know that?" I asked.

"I telephoned from Southampton," he replied, "and Miss Macey said you hadn't come back and that Bariatinsky was furious."

"I went ... home," I repeated.

"I had no idea you had left London," David said, "so I sent my telegrams and letters to the Boarding House."

"You wrote to me?"

"Nearly every day."

"I wish I had known."

"I think it was one of the biggest shocks of my life," David continued, "when the woman showed me all my letters to you unopened and done up in bundles with elastic bands round them. She had telephoned Giles to ask him where she should send them, but he didn't know either where you were."

127

"I meant to write after I got home and say I wasn't coming back."

"Eventually he went down to the Vicarage to find you, as I did, when I returned to England," David said, "but you had disappeared."

"You went to the Vicarage!" I exclaimed incredulously.

"Giles told me where you lived and I couldn't believe you wouldn't be there," he answered. "But there was a new incumbent – a pompous old fool who told me your father had died weeks before he moved in, and as far as I could make out he didn't even know you existed."

"Why should he?" I asked weakly.

"Where were you?" David questioned. "I asked a woman called Mrs. Harris who did say you had gone with a lady who came to the funeral."

"That was Aunt Lucy," I said. "My father's sister."

"And where does she live?"

"Near Southampton," I answered. "She is the Mother Superior of a Convent."

"A Convent?"

There was no doubt of the surprise in David's voice.

"You see," I began, "two days after I got home Daddy . . . died of a . . . heart-attack."

Reflection 18

It sounded such a cold explanation spoken like that, and it was impossible to explain, even to David, what a shock I had when I walked into the Vicarage and found Daddy looking so ill that it was almost difficult to recognise him.

"What have you been doing to yourself?" I asked.

"I have had some rather unpleasant pain lately," he answered. "I thought it was indigestion and Dr. Mackintosh gave me some white mixture, but it hasn't helped very much."

I was horrified not only at his appearance but also at the condition of the Vicarage. I had never seen such a mess.

Mrs. Harris was never a good worker, and although the kitchen was fairly clean the rest of the house was dusty, dirty and untidy.

Because I hadn't been there, there had been no-one to put away the Church magazines, the prayer-books used by the choir, or even the things left over from the Bazaar which were still in the Hall, where the stall-holders had dumped them.

Daddy's study was thick with dust, the ashes needed raking out of the fireplace, and I don't think his shoes had had a brush or a polish for weeks.

As I had arrived at supper-time I went into the kitchen to see what Mrs. Harris had left for him, but all I could find was a plate of cold mince which not only looked but smelt unappetising.

There was nothing else except for a few eggs from the chickens in the garden with which I made an omelette.

He ate it nervously because he kept saying he was sure it would bring on his pains again.

"I'm going to send for Dr. Mackintosh in the morning and insist upon his sending you to a Specialist in Cheltenham or Worcester," I said. "You can't go on like this."

I didn't want to frighten him, but he seemed to have aged by years since the last time I had seen him and there was a look about his face I didn't like.

I also noticed when we went upstairs to bed that he found it difficult to breathe.

Because she didn't know I was coming back, Mrs. Harris

hadn't bothered to change the sheets on my bed and the room certainly hadn't been aired since I went away.

It smelt musty, so I opened the windows and when I looked out on to the quiet and peace of the garden I thought of David on the *Queen Mary* sailing to America, and I told myself my life was over.

I wished I had never gone to London and I thought perhaps all that had happened was a punishment because I hadn't stayed at home to look after Daddy.

But I didn't cry. I still felt numb inside; a horrible heavy numbness which made me feel as if I was watching somebody not really myself, move about and talk.

I got up in the morning and started to clean the house. At nine o'clock I sent a boy down to the village to ask Dr. Mackintosh to come up and see Daddy.

I gave the boy tuppence to run the errand and he came back an hour later to say that Dr. Mackintosh was away until Sunday evening.

This was something I hadn't expected: people seldom went away at Little Poolbrook. But I knew there was nothing I could do except wait for his return and then insist that Daddy should see a Specialist.

When Mrs. Harris came I sent her off to the Butcher to get a leg of lamb and I cooked Daddy a really good lunch.

He just sat in his study and I could see he felt too ill even to walk round the garden. I wondered what I ought to do about the Church Services the next day, because I felt certain he wasn't well enough to hold Communion in the morning or to take matins at eleven o'clock.

He had some lunch and seemed a little brighter, and at about five o'clock he told me he thought he would go to bed.

"I'll go and get it ready for you," I said, "and I'll bring up your dinner."

"I don't want any, thank you," he answered.

"I insist on your having something," I said firmly. "And,

Daddy, don't you think I had better go and see the old Rector and ask him if he'll take the Services for you to-morrow?"

The old Rector was very old indeed. After serving in a Parish the other side of Worcester, he had retired to a small cottage on the edge of our village, and sometimes during Christmas and Easter he would help Daddy with the Services.

He was, however, over eighty and his hands were very shaky.

"I'll manage," Daddy said firmly.

"I don't think you ought to," I argued.

"No, I want to go to Church," he said. "It is your mother's birthday next week, Samantha, and I always say special prayers for her both the Sunday before and the Sunday after."

At that moment I wished, as I had never wished before, that Mummy was with me. I felt worried not only about Daddy but also about myself.

I had thought on the way home that perhaps I would tell Daddy about David, but when I saw how ill he looked I knew I couldn't worry him with my troubles.

"Why have you come home, Samantha?" he had asked.

"I've been given a few days' holiday," I answered, "and I thought you would like to see me."

"Of course I want to see you," he said. "You look very pretty – very pretty indeed, Samantha. Are you enjoying your job?"

'Yes," I lied, "but it's lovely to be home."

This wasn't the moment, I felt, to tell him I wasn't going back, that I could never face London again.

I expected to lie awake all night thinking of David. Instead I slept from sheer exhaustion. I awoke to hear myself call out his name because I had dreamt he was sailing away from me down a silver river in the moonlight.

'He's sailing away, all right,' I told myself.

I wondered if he had slept last night in Lady Bettine's bed and felt sure he had.

I heard Daddy getting up, so I went downstairs and made him a cup of tea. He usually wouldn't eat or drink anything before Communion, but this morning I insisted on his having the tea.

He raised no objections, so I felt he knew he needed it.

He sat down at the kitchen-table to drink the tea although I had meant to carry it into the study. When he finished he said:

"Thank you, Samantha. I hoped you would come to Church this morning."

I was just going to answer him when he gave a sudden cry, clutched at his chest and collapsed on the floor.

I knelt down beside him and tried to loosen his collar, but it was difficult because it fastened at the back. Then as I touched him I knew he was dead!

Reflection 19

"I'm sorry about your father," David said in a quiet voice beside me.

"It happened so quickly," I answered. "And I suppose it was shock that made me behave as I did after the funeral."

"What did you do?" he asked.

"I couldn't stop crying," I answered. "I just cried and cried, and Aunt Lucy, who was the only relation to whom I sent a telegram about Daddy, took me away with her."

"To the Convent?"

"I didn't realise it was a Convent for some time."

"Why not?"

"I think I had a kind of brain-storm," I answered, "or perhaps it was a nervous breakdown, I don't know. But whatever it was they only stopped me crying by keeping me more or less unconscious."

"Poor Samantha," David said. "I suppose I am at least partly to blame for that."

"I think it was everything happening at once," I answered. "After all, you and Daddy were the only people in the whole world I had to love."

There was silence for a moment and then David said:

"Go on with your story, Samantha, I want to know exactly what happened."

His voice was gentle and because we were alone in the dark I found it easy to talk in a manner which would have been far more difficult any other time.

Not being able to see David, but knowing he was there, was comforting; and yet, at the same time, it was almost as he had been in my dreams.

Always when we had been together before I had been afraid of saying the wrong things, showing my ignorance, or just upsetting him.

I expect it was because he was such an overpowering and vital personality that by contrast I felt insignificant and insecure.

But now because it was dark we were both as it were, disembodied, so that I felt able to talk to David as I had always wanted to, as if we were equal.

So I began telling him how when I became conscious I had found that the Nun looking after me was French.

She was a refugee who had escaped from France when the Germans were advancing on Paris and she hadn't gone back after the War.

She told me that 'The Order of the Little Sisters of Mary' were Teaching-Nuns, and there was a school attached to the Convent where she taught French.

I thought about this after she had left me to go to sleep and when she came back I said:

"Sister Thérèse, will you teach me to speak French? I know a little, but I'm sure I have a terrible accent and no grammar."

She was delighted at the idea and she insisted that I always spoke French to her whenever she came to my room.

It was then that the idea came to me that I must change myself into being what David wanted. He had said I was 'abysmally ignorant' and of course it was true.

My education, I realised, had been lamentable. I had been sent to Worcester High School for about three years, but my attendance had been very spasmodic.

If there was something extra to do at the Vicarage I stayed at home. Also, if the weather was bad I would find it difficult to get to school.

The Station on the direct line to Worcester was three miles away and the only method of getting there was by bicycle.

In the summer I rather enjoyed the ride but in the winter when it was pouring with rain, or snowing, or there were strong winds, I dreaded having to bicycle off early in the morning and bicycle home when it was growing dark.

I think Mummy worried about my going alone in the train. She was always very insistent that I must find a carriage marked 'Ladies Only', and she made me promise that when I arrived at Worcester Station I wouldn't hang about but hurry as quickly as I could to the High School.

Anyway, what with one thing and another, I have a suspicion I was absent from school more times than I was present.

Before this I had a Governess who had retired to live in a tiny cottage in Little Poolbrook which she had inherited from a relative.

She was very old, rather disagreeable, and she used to get very cross when I didn't understand what she told me the first time she said it. So rather than upset her, I would often pretend to have grasped the subject when I really had only the vaguest idea of what she had been trying to teach me.

I suppose if we had owned an extensive Library I would have read lots of books. But apart from a set of Dickens and one of Sir Walter Scott's novels, most of the books in Daddy's study were bound sermons or religious treatises which I found extremely dull.

Often Daddy would read extracts from the newspapers to Mummy in the evenings when she was sewing or embroidering, which she did so well, but I cannot say from that that my general knowledge was much to boast about.

In fact, David was right in everything he said about me, and perhaps that was what had made me so angry.

No-one really likes hearing the truth about oneself.

Lying in my bed in the little room in the Convent which was really one of the Nun's cells, I made up my mind that I would start to educate myself.

When Aunt Lucy came to see me I told her what I intended, and because she was so glad I was taking an interest in something and no longer crying, she went to a great deal of trouble.

She got Sister Magdalene, the Nun who taught Literature and History, to advise me what to read and she would bring me all the books she thought would help me.

Surprisingly the Nuns had quite a large Library, and although naturally there were no modern novels, and they would not have thought of including David's book, there were lots of the Classics.

There was Thackeray, Jane Austen and Trollope, to

mention but a few, and Sister Magdalene gave me books on Mythology which I enjoyed more than anything else.

The Doctor insisted that I must rest, so I lay in bed and read. When he let me get up I would sit in the garden, which was very peaceful, and go on reading.

When I didn't understand anything I discussed it with Sister Magdalene, and every day I talked to Sister Thérèse in French until she seemed really pleased with me.

Gradually I got stronger although I still found it difficult to eat, and the food at the Convent was not very tempting.

One day Aunt Lucy came out into the garden and said to me:

"Don't you think, Samantha, that it's time you returned to work?"

I looked at her in surprise. I had got so used to thinking of myself as an invalid that I really hadn't realised that sooner or later I would have to either go back to London and Giles or find other employment.

Aunt Lucy had already told me that Daddy had left me everything he possessed, which wasn't very much – just a few hundred pounds. Enough to keep me from starving, but I would certainly have to earn my own living for the rest of my life.

Somehow it was a shock to think that Aunt Lucy wanted to get rid of me.

"Do you want me to go away?" I asked.

"No, Samantha, I like having you here," Aunt Lucy replied, "but you cannot spend the rest of your life doing nothing but read. You are young and this is not the right sort of existence for a young girl."

"Some of the Nuns are as young as I am," I argued.

"Do you want to become a Nun?" Aunt Lucy enquired.

I thought of David and knew that that was the last thing I wanted. I wanted to see him again, I wanted him to love me as he had done before he realised how very inadequate I was.

Unfortunately, learning had only made me realise how much more I had to learn.

I suppose I had always known I was ignorant, but only when I began to study properly, was I appalled to find how little I knew. There were great blank spaces in my mind which ought to have been filled with History and Geography and a knowledge of world events.

"There is so much I want to do here, Aunt Lucy," I said.

She didn't answer and I found out later she had telephoned Giles and told him where I was.

He had, it appeared, been very worried by my disappearance, although he had thought at first that I must have gone home. Anyway he said he would like me back, and he said the same to me when Aunt Lucy made me telephone him.

"*Vogue* and a number of other papers are asking particularly for pictures of you, Samantha," he said. "You've made it very difficult for me running off in that irresponsible manner."

"I'm sorry," I said meekly.

"Your Aunt tells me you have been very unhappy over your father's death," Giles went on, "and of course in the circumstances, I must forgive you. But come back at once, Samantha. There is a lot of work to be done."

I went back to London feeling nervous and rather frightened, not only of Giles but also in case I met David.

"I'll come back only on one condition," I said to Giles on the telephone, "and that is you don't ask David Durham to the Studio while I am there, and that you don't give him my new address."

"Don't you wish to see him?" Giles asked in surprise.

"No!" I replied briefly.

There was a silence as if he was thinking over what I had said and then he answered:

"Your private life is nothing to do with me, Samantha. If you don't want to see David Durham, I shall certainly not tell him where you are living."

When Giles saw me he was delighted that I had grown so thin.

Personally, I think I am all eyes with no face, and Melanie teases me for looking like a lamp-post. But Edward Molyneux and Norman Hartnell were thrilled and promised to design several dresses especially for me in their new collections.

One of the first things I did on getting back to London was to join a Library, and after a week or so they got used to my changing my books every other day and would joke about it when I appeared.

I was doing my best about my education, but I had not forgotten that David also said I was 'absurdly innocent'!

I could still hear him saying the words in that scathing, sarcastic voice which always seemed to flick me on the raw and make me feel miserable.

I thought of him with Lady Bettine and I knew that all the women who had hung around him in the past and whom perhaps he had loved, had been sophisticated and very, very experienced.

It was not surprising, I told myself miserably, that he found me boring. How could I be anything else when I was as ignorant about love as I was about everything else?

The difficulty was that while I could read History and Literature and other subjects, there didn't seem to be a book to teach me about love.

I had, of course, while I was reading, learnt of the great love-affairs down the centuries, and when I thought about it I came to the conclusion that if I really loved David I had been wrong not to do what he wanted.

After all, Kings had given up their thrones, countries had gone to war, families had engaged in endless vendettas, men had been tortured or died for love!

Women had sacrificed their reputations, their children, their status in society, and even their lives, because they loved a man to the exclusion of all else.

Perhaps David was right and love was too important for us to refuse it.

I thought and thought about David and how he had wanted me to go away with him. It seemed to me the more I read, the more I found that people were prepared to make a sacrifice of everything they held dear, if it was for someone they loved.

It took me a long time to think it out and then I told myself that if I loved David enough I must do as he wanted, however much it might be against my principles.

I kept feeling that to win him back I personally had to make a sacrifice, and that nothing was too difficult or too frightening to do if it would make David love me again.

I lay awake night after night planning how the day would come when I would go to David and say:

"I'm no longer 'abysmally ignorant' nor am I 'absurdly innocent'. I now know quite a lot, and I am experienced in love."

And then in my imagination he would hold out his arms and tell me that he loved me and we would be happy again.

Even to think of David holding me close and kissing me made me feel a little of that ecstasy and wonder he had given me when I first knew him.

It seemed a very long time ago, but there was one thing that was comforting and that was to know that, if he would not marry me, David was unlikely to marry anyone else.

'Perhaps when he sees how different I have become and realises how hard I have worked because I love him, he will ask me to be his wife,' I told myself.

Even as I did so I felt it was only a dream, an impossible, fantastic dream, which would never come true! But I had to try!

I had to struggle and fight to change myself simply because, as I said to myself, "Without David I will never be happy again and there will be no reason to go on living."

I heard my voice die away in the darkness. I seemed to have been talking for a very long time.

I had concentrated so hard in recalling what had happened that as I talked I had almost forgotten that David was really there and was listening.

It had been like talking to the imaginary David as I had done every night since I had run away from him.

I started when suddenly he said in his deep voice:

"What happened then, Samantha?"

"I met . . . Peter and . . . Victor . . ." I answered.

"Tell me about them," David ordered.

Reflection 20

Melanie, Hortense and I had been taken by Giles to Syon House, which belonged to the Duke of Northumberland, to be photographed.

Vogue had the idea of having models posed against realistic backgrounds in famous houses.

Syon House was fantastic! I had never realised a house could be so beautiful and so elegant.

I wish I could have seen it in the old days when it had dozens of flunkeys in their silver-buttoned livery and the Duke had given grand parties attended by Royalty.

The house had been shut up for most of the War and it had a slightly un-lived-in look which houses get when the family who own it are not in residence. But it was still breath-taking to look at and I really enjoyed posing in the pillared Hall, with its gilded statues, in the Long Gallery and the beautiful Salons.

Giles had finished with me for the moment and was concentrating on Melanie and Hortense, so I wandered away to look at the pictures.

I was standing in front of a very beautiful Dutch painting when I heard someone approach.

I thought it was Giles and I said:

"I wonder who painted this?"

"Jan Van Eyck," a man's voice answered, and I looked round in surprise.

It was not Giles as I had expected, but a fair-haired man of about thirty, bare-headed and carrying a large notebook.

He was obviously a gentleman and I thought he might be one of the Northumberland family.

"Are you interested in pictures?" he asked.

"I wish I knew more about them," I answered, thinking once again how ignorant I was, and here was another subject about which I knew nothing.

"Would you like me to tell you what I know?" he asked.

"Would you do that?"

He smiled.

"I know who you are, so perhaps I should introduce myself. My name is Peter Sinclair."

"Are you a relation of the Duke?" I asked ingenuously.

He laughed.

"Nothing so grand. I work at Christies. I am here to revalue some of the pictures and furniture. The Duke thinks they are under-insured."

I knew that Christies were the famous auctioneers in St. James's Street who held auctions of pictures and antique furniture.

"You must have a very interesting job," I said.

"Perhaps it is almost as interesting as yours," he answered. "Let me tell you about the pictures and you will then be able to tell me if they are as absorbing as the lovely gowns you wear."

We walked around the Gallery and he told me the most fascinating stories, not only about the pictures but also the artists who painted them, and how they had come into the possession of the Northumberland family.

There was something about Peter I liked the moment I met him.

He was very quiet and unassuming, and he told me afterwards it was the bravest thing he had ever done in speaking to me and offering to be my guide.

"I'm really a very shy person, Samantha," he said, "but I had the feeling that you were anxious to learn and that made me brave."

I suppose it was again brave of him, when Giles said it was time to leave, to ask me if I would like to go with him the next day, which happened to be Saturday, to a house in the country where he had to inspect some furniture which was being sent to Christies to be auctioned.

It was the first of many houses Peter took me to, and because he loved antiques he made me love them too.

I learnt all sorts of interesting things from him which I am sure no-one else would have told me and which never appear in the guide-books.

For instance how Van Dyke painted hands better than anybody else; how Grinley Gibbons always put an ear of corn among his carvings as a kind of trade mark; how Botticelli's model for the 'Birth of Venus' had died at the age of twenty-three of consumption and had been so beautiful that great crowds had stood silent in the street to watch her coffin pass.

Peter made the things he talked about come to life and I

became more and more fascinated with everything he told me.

"This," I told myself, "is the proper way to learn and I am sure that everything that seems new to me, David has known all his life."

Then gradually I thought perhaps he could teach me more than just about pictures and furniture.

When I first made up my mind that to please David I must be experienced in love, I realised, of course, it meant becoming involved with a man.

The mere idea of letting someone like Lord Rowden touch me made me feel sick.

I had managed to avoid seeing him since I had come back to London. I hoped that after I had behaved so badly at his house-party and made him look a fool by running away, he would not wish to speak to me again, but Melanie told me that he had enquired after me several times before my return.

I knew I could not bear Lord Rowden even to come near me, let alone kiss me, but there had to be a man somewhere that I could tolerate, otherwise I would go on being 'absurdly innocent' and a 'crashing bore' for ever.

Of course, all the usual young men had turned up again to ask me out to dinner and to dance. But when I could avoid Giles knowing about it, I refused every invitation and went home alone at night to get on with my reading.

I had made up my mind that I couldn't face the Boarding House again. It was not only because it was so uncomfortable, but because I felt Mrs. Simpson might ask questions.

So I went to a cheap Hotel for the first week, and then a House-Agent found me my flat. It was small but I could just afford the rent and I could put in it some of the furniture from the Vicarage which I had left in store.

It was quite an effort to get it ready, but Peter found me a very cheap painter to work after hours and who charged far less than a firm would have done.

I altered the curtains myself to fit the windows and Peter hung the pictures for me.

They weren't great masters like those we had looked at in other people's houses; but I had known them all my life, and I loved having them with me as a reminder of Mummy and Daddy. I knew that in a way they prevented me from being lonely.

Even when Peter gave me dinner he never suggested coming into the flat at night. I knew he was thinking of my reputation and was afraid of my being talked about by the other tenants in the house.

He was also kind and understanding and ready to listen to what I had to say. He never laughed at me for not knowing the right answer and he never got cross or irritable if I forgot something he had already told me.

It took me a little time, but finally I made up my mind that when Peter wanted to kiss me, as he was sure to do sooner or later – the young Guardsmen were still trying to do so every time they took me out – I would say 'yes'.

Then, I supposed, like David, he would want to make love to me and I would say 'yes' to that too.

I tried not to feel that I would shrink away and feel horrified when the moment came.

After all, I liked Peter, I liked him very much indeed. He was the kindest and nicest friend I ever had and he was so gentle that I really didn't think that he would frighten anyone, not even me.

The extraordinary thing was that Peter didn't try to kiss me, and although he asked me out almost every evening and took me to the country every Saturday, he was just friendly kind and sympathetic as he had always been.

If it hadn't been for all the other young men who were endlessly asking me to go out dancing with them, and who made veiled innuendos about other things we might do, would have begun to feel I had lost all my attractions.

"I must give Peter more encouragement," I told myself. "If we go on at this rate I shall be one hundred and thirty before I am experienced enough for David, by which time he will have forgotten all about me."

I couldn't think of David and Lady Bettine without feeling that terrible, agonising pain inside me which had taken the place of the numb misery that I had felt when I had known they were going to be together on the *Queen Mary*.

I tried not to think about them but it was very difficult; for I kept seeing them clinging together as they danced at Bray Park, Lady Bettine's slanting eyes looking up into David's and her red lips inviting his.

"Oh, David ... David ..." I would cry inside me and I would force myself to think of something else.

It was only sometimes at night I really cried because it seemed so hopeless. Then I would tell myself that I hadn't given my plan a proper chance and there was Peter only waiting for me to suggest that we made love together.

I wasn't quite certain what that entailed but I thought that perhaps with Peter it wouldn't be too horrifying.

Then one evening when we came back from the country having had a delicious dinner just outside London, Peter drove me back to the flat and said:

"Can I come in for a moment, Samantha?"

For the moment I was too surprised to answer him. He had never suggested it before. Then I knew this was what I had been waiting for.

"Yes ... of course, Peter," I answered after a moment's pause.

I got out of the car and waited while he locked up and then he followed me up the steps.

I felt so nervous I could hardly open my flat door.

The room looked very nice and cosy and Peter had given me some roses which scented the air.

Peter shut the door behind him and I stood still, thinking that he would take me in his arms and kiss me for the first time.

My lips felt dry and I had an idiotic desire to run away and lock myself in my Bed-room.

"I want to talk to you, Samantha," Peter said quietly.

"Yes, of course," I said. "Shall we sit down?"

I sat down on the sofa which was really too big for the room and Peter sat beside me.

I thought he would take my hand but after a moment he said:

"I want to tell you, Samantha, that I'm going away."

"Going away?" I ejaculated in astonishment.

"I'm going to Italy," he said. "Christies have some work to do there and when they suggested I should do it, I accepted."

"Will you be away long?" I asked.

"That rather depends," Peter answered. "You see, Samantha, I'm going away because of you!"

"Because of me?" I echoed in surprise.

He looked away from me and I thought he seemed very tense.

"The fact is, Samantha, I've fallen in love with you."

"Is there anything wrong in that?" I asked.

"Yes, as far as you are concerned," he replied.

My eyes widened and he said still without looking at me:

"You see, Samantha, I love you because I think you are the most wonderful, adorable person I have ever met in my life, and I would give everything I possess to be able to ask you to marry me."

I drew in my breath, but I really didn't know what to say.

"But I can't ask you," Peter went on, "because it wouldn' be fair to you."

"Why not?" I enquired.

"Because, Samantha, I was wounded in the War," Peter said, "not very seriously, but the Doctors say it is very unlikely that I could ever have children."

"Oh ... Peter ..." I murmured.

"I've never worried about it particularly," Peter went on, "because until now I have never wanted to marry anybody. But you are perfect in every way, Samantha, and it wouldn't be fair for you to miss what I know for a woman is perhaps the most important experience in her life – having a baby."

"Are ... you sure they ... were right?" I asked hesitatingly.

"Quite sure about that," Peter said. "That's not to say that I couldn't make love to you, but I couldn't face the day, Samantha, when you would reproach me because you would feel that I had deprived you of something that is every woman's right. So I'm going away."

"Oh ... Peter ... Peter!" I cried.

It was all so unexpected, something I had never dreamt might happen, and I didn't know what to say, I could only put out my hands towards him.

He took them in his and raised them to his lips one after the other. Then he rose to his feet.

"You are very beautiful, Samantha," he said, "not only because of your lovely face, but you are nice, kind and completely unspoilt. I hope that one day we will be able to be friends again, but in the meantime I shall pass through a very unpleasant hell on my own until I can get used to not seeing you."

"But ... you mustn't go away ... like this ..." I began.

He put two fingers on my lips to stop me speaking.

"Don't say it, Samantha," he said. "We both know that I am doing the right thing; for while I'm in love with you, you are not in love with me. Just take care of yourself and I only hope the young man over whom you are breaking your heart is worthy of you."

I was absolutely astonished at this, because I had never mentioned David to him and I had no idea that Peter knew I was in love or, as he said, breaking my heart.

He walked towards the door, then he turned suddenly.

He took me in his arms and held me very close to him. I thought he would kiss my lips but instead he kissed my forehead, and before I could say anything or even hold on to him, he opened the door.

I stood where he had left me and heard his car start up. I tried to realise that Peter had gone out of my life for ever.

I was so sorry for him and wished I could have told him how much he meant to me! I knew that now he had gone away there would be an empty place in my life and there was no-one else at hand to fill it.

For the next few days I tried to forget Peter by going out with anyone who asked me.

I danced at the Savoy, at the Berkeley, at the Embassy Club on Thursday night, and at the Kit-Kat.

Every place seemed to be full of the same people dancing to the same music and, it seemed to me, saying the same things over and over again.

"You're looking bored, Samantha," a young man said to me one night and I thought perhaps I was beginning to look like all the other fashionable women. I wondered if David would think that an improvement or not.

Now that Peter had gone I had to start all over again finding someone to teach me about love.

I would sometimes look round the restaurant or the club and instead of finding the men attractive I could only compare them with David and think how stupid and ordinary they were.

None of them had his presence, his personality or th

vitality that seemed to exude from him, so that the moment he walked into a room people noticed him.

I was at a party at the Savoy one evening. It was a rather noisy, tiresome party. Several of the men had had too much to drink and ragged about during the cabaret which I always think is very bad manners.

They also danced rather rowdily, which was not only embarrassing, but worried me in case my dress was torn.

The party was given for a very rich Argentine. We had sat down twenty-four to dinner and then after the theatres closed other friends kept arriving to join us.

I cannot remember how I got invited – I think it must have been through Giles. It was the sort of party I hate and I was wondering how soon I could slip away and go home when three men arrived.

Two of them were nondescript and looked like all the other men present, but the third was definitely different.

He was dark and very good-looking, almost outstandingly so, and the moment he appeared everyone seemed to wake up and get interested.

"Victor!" a woman cried. "Where have you been, darling? I haven't seen you for ages!"

Our host also greeted him most effusively, and as he sat down at the table it seemed as if the whole tempo had risen and everyone was talking animatedly and excitedly all at once.

"Who is that?" I asked the man sitting next to me.

"Don't you know Victor Fitzroy?" he replied. "I thought everyone knew Victor."

"Everyone but me," I answered.

"Well, he is certainly somebody you ought to meet," my dinner-partner said quite seriously. "I can't understand how you haven't already read about him in the newspapers."

"I never have time to read the gossip-columns," I answered.

"I was talking about the headlines," he said. "I always tell Victor he hogs them so that none of us can get a look in."

"What does he do?" I asked.

"It would be easier to tell you what he doesn't do," my informant replied. "He has just beaten the air-speed record from Capetown to London. He has won all sorts of motor-car racing trophies and is one of the best amateur riders in England."

"Obviously a very talented gentleman!" I laughed.

"He is also enormously rich! However, if you don't appreciate Victor Fitzroy for himself you won't appreciate anybody."

A few minutes later I had the chance to judge, for it seemed that Victor had noticed me across the table since our host brought him over to introduce him.

"Come and dance," Victor suggested and I was delighted to agree.

I was rather intrigued by a man about whom another man talked with such enthusiasm, and I found very quickly that my dinner-partner had not exaggerated.

Victor had tremendous charm, almost too much in a way. It was overwhelming.

He didn't pay me the usual compliments, he just said:

"The moment I saw you I knew why I was in such a hurry to get back to England last week."

"Why do you want to fly so quickly?" I asked.

He laughed at that.

"I hate wasting time," he said. "If I want something I want it at once."

He looked at me as he spoke with a sort of speculative look in his eyes. Then he said:

"Tell me about yourself."

"I expect you have already been told I am a Giles Bariatinsky model?"

"I am not interested in the advertising slogans but in what lies behind them."

He held me really close to him and said:

"You are very thin."

"I'm sorry if I disappoint you," I answered.

"You don't," he said. "I am really wondering if you are real, or if you will disappear at the touch of a hand."

"I think that depends on whose hand," I answered.

I realised I was flirting in a manner I was seldom able to do with other men.

There was something effervescent about Victor. He made one feel gay and amusing. He made one sparkle, just as he sparkled himself.

We danced and danced until he said:

"Let's go – my car is outside."

"Without saying good-bye and expressing our thanks?"

"Our host should thank you. People must pay you to sit at their dull and boring dinner-parties and look beautiful. You are far more effective than floral decorations."

"Thank you," I laughed.

I did as Victor wanted and walked out of the Savoy without saying good-bye.

I realised later that it was the way people expected Victor Fitzroy to behave. They were grateful if he accepted their hospitality, even for a few moments.

He had a long low expensive sports car outside the Savoy and we raced down the Strand through Trafalgar Square and passed Buckingham Palace at such a speed that I was only surprised we weren't stopped by the police.

"Do you really want to go home?" Victor asked.

"I'm afraid I must," I answered. "I'm a working girl, and I get into trouble if I'm late in the morning."

"I will let you go only on condition that you promise to dine with me to-morrow night."

"I would love to," I answered.

"I have a feeling we are going to see a lot of each other, Samantha," Victor said, "so like you, I won't waste time on unnecessary preliminaries."

"Are you trying to say that I should have refused your first invitation?" I asked.

"I'm telling you," he answered, "that I would not have allowed you to do so."

When we reached my flat I was ready to step out quickly as I always did but I found it difficult to open the car door.

Victor helped me out and took my keys from me.

He opened both doors and then he walked into my flat before I could stop him.

I stood looking at him speculatively, then he put his arms round me and said:

"You are very lovely, Samantha!"

He kissed me before I could move or make any effort to prevent him, but surprisingly it didn't shock or frighten me. Then as suddenly as he had taken me in his arms, Victor let me go.

"I shall be looking forward to to-morrow, my sweet," he said and left me.

I felt as if I was in a whirl. I didn't know quite what I thought or didn't think. It was just as if I had been swept off my feet and carried along on a tide over which I had no control.

It was not an unpleasant feeling, it was rather fun, and I told myself as I locked the door and turned out the light in the Sitting-room that I liked Victor.

I was looking forward to to-morrow evening.

'To-night,' I thought, 'instead of thinking of David, I'll think about Victor!'

The following night I took an extra amount of trouble, choosing one of my prettiest dresses. I had my hair done at lunchtime, and I was ready a quarter of an hour before I expected Victor to arrive.

I might have known that when he did come it would be somewhat flamboyantly.

There was the noise of his car outside and then he seemed, as I opened the door, to sweep into the flat like a boisterous wind.

He was smiling and I thought he really was one of the best-looking men I had ever seen.

He put his hands on my shoulders and held me away from him.

"Let me look at you," he said. "I thought last night I really had dreamt you – no-one could be quite so beautiful."

"What do you think now?" I asked.

"I'm sure you are a fake," he said, "but I've got to find out for certain."

"That's not very complimentary," I said accusingly.

"You've had enough compliments," he said, "but just to spoil you I will say you are entrancing, and I would much rather kiss you than have that drink you haven't offered me."

He held me close to him and kissed my lips.

"I'm sorry," I said when he released me, "but I haven't any drink."

"Are all your boy-friends teetotallers?" he asked.

"I haven't any."

"You can hardly expect me to believe that."

"The men I do know," I replied, "are not allowed into my flat."

I picked up my wrap as I spoke and moved towards the door.

Victor looked round.

"The setting is not really worthy of the jewel," he said.

I felt I ought to have been angry with him for being critical, but one didn't get angry with Victor over small things.

"It is what I like."

"And that's all that matters," he replied. "At least you are not pretentious, Samantha."

"I hope not."

He led me to the car and we roared away to the West End. A table had been kept for him at the Embassy Club where, of course, he knew everybody.

People came up and talked to him; he waved to his friends across the room, and it was rather like being out with a film-star.

In between the interruptions he made love to me amusingly, and with that quite irresistible charm which made me certain I oughtn't to believe a word of it.

But he was so skilful at it that I found him fascinating.

From the Embassy we went on to a nightclub where there was an extra-ordinarily amusing cabaret, and then to a small, dark, seductive cellar where one danced on a glass floor lit from beneath and sat at small velvet-covered sofa-tables which were very intimate.

Victor talked to me beguilingly and in a manner that in some way healed the wound to my pride.

David had not only made me miserably unhappy; he had left me humble and insecure, deflated and insignificant.

I can't explain what Victor did except that I felt as if he lifted me up out of the gutter and placed me on a pedestal.

I felt young and gay again, I felt the world was not a place of misery and oppression, but of laughter and sunshine.

We talked and danced and it was nearly dawn before he drove me home.

Once again he came into the flat and kissed me more passionately than he had done the night before and left me just as suddenly, while I was still willing for him to go on kissing me.

It was the next night, after we had been to the theatre and were having supper at the Savoy, that he said:

"I've a suggestion to make to you, Samantha."

"What is it?" I asked.

"I want to go to Paris to-morrow morning," he said, "Will you come with me?"

For a moment I could think of nothing to say and then I knew that this was what I had been waiting for; what I had envisaged would happen sooner or later; and it would be stupid for me to refuse.

I liked Victor, I liked him enormously. I loved being with him. I thought I had never laughed or enjoyed anything so much as I had these last two nights.

But Paris . . .!

Then as I thought about it, Victor put his hand over mine.

"Say yes, Samantha," he said. "I want you to come with me, and I'm not going to take 'no' for an answer."

Reflection 21

I stopped talking and waited for David to say something but there was only silence, and after a moment, because I didn't want to discuss what I had been saying, I went on with my story.

It was difficult to explain what I felt as I drove down to Croydon Aerodrome with Victor.

I was excited at the thought of going to Paris. At the same time I was conscious of a funny, sick feeling inside me which I always have before a big party.

I kept telling myself I had to be sensible and carry out the plan I had made when I was at the Convent.

I loved David and this was the only way I could make him

155

love me again and find me desirable, as he had when we had first known each other.

The more I thought about it, the more I realised how boring I must have been to him understanding only about half of what he was saying to me and having no knowledge of anything outside the narrow world of Little Poolbrook.

I felt, although it was only a drop in the ocean, that I had learnt a little since he went to America, both from reading and from Peter, and now here was Victor, so charming, so gay, to teach me about love.

I kept telling myself I was very lucky. Nevertheless, as the day wore on the sick feeling seemed to intensify even though I tried not to think about it.

It was very exciting when we reached Croydon to find that we were to travel to Paris in Victor's own Puss-Moth, which was outside the hangar awaiting us when we arrived.

All the Officials seemed very impressed with Victor and congratulated him on winning the race from Capetown to London, and I could see that the mechanics looked at him with admiration.

It was the first time I had ever flown and once we were in the air Victor turned to me with a smile and said:

"You're not frightened, are you, Samantha?"

"Not now," I answered, "although I couldn't help being afraid that you would never get this big bird off the ground."

He laughed at that and took one hand off the controls to pat mine and say:

"You're quite safe with me and I can't imagine anything more fun than being up in the clouds with you."

It was fun for me too and the world seemed far away, almost like a child's toy, as we flew over England and then over the Channel.

The aeroplane was noisy so it wasn't easy to talk, and when we got into the clouds there wasn't much to see.

It was only when we were coming down that I felt frightened again: the world seemed at first far away and then came towards us in a rush, and I couldn't see why we wouldn't hit it with a tremendous bang and both be killed.

But Victor brought the Moth down smoothly and we only bumped a little before he brought it to a standstill.

A large car was waiting for us when we climbed out and we were swept away from Le Bourget towards Paris.

Victor took my hand in the car and said:

"Happy, Samantha?"

"Very!" I replied.

It wasn't quite true, but I must have sounded convincing because he said:

"I want you to be thrilled with Paris. To me it is the most fascinating city in the world, and the only possible place for lovers."

That made me wonder if I would ever go to Paris with David, and when I saw how beautiful the city was, I longed to have him there.

We passed The Opera which was very impressive and then drove down a street which Victor told me was the Rue de la Paix, which led into the Place Vendôme, with its high column in the centre.

"Where are we staying?" I enquired, thinking it was a question I might have asked sooner.

"The Ritz," Victor answered casually. "I always stay there."

He greeted the Concierge and the reception clerks as if they were old friends, and we were taken upstairs to a most attractive suite overlooking a quiet garden with a huge Bedroom and bathroom for me and the same for Victor, with a Sitting-room in between.

There were flowers everywhere, and when the porters had brought up our luggage and Victor had tipped them he kissed me lightly and said:

"Come on, Samantha, let's go and enjoy ourselves."

I lost count by the end of the evening of all the places Victor took me to, but wherever he went he seemed to find friends.

There were bars, restaurants, a special place in the Bois where we had drinks, and when we had changed we dined at the most fascinating place called Maxim's, which was very like the Embassy Club.

Victor knew half the people in the room, and after a superlative dinner we danced to the best Band I have ever heard.

After that we went to a nightclub in Montmartre, where there was a cabaret and the girls wore very few clothes.

We had only been there a little time before Victor said:

"This is boring. Let's go home, Samantha."

It was then I felt again a funny, cold feeling inside me as to what lay ahead.

Victor had been so interesting. We had talked so intimately of so many things and we had met so many different people that I really hadn't had a moment to worry about myself or what was going to happen when we were alone.

It was only when I began to undress in my Bed-room in the Ritz that I wondered why I was there and if I had been crazy to accept Victor's invitation.

For the first time I realised that he must have taken it for granted that I was sophisticated and experienced.

It was not only the way I looked and that I was a Giles Bariatinsky model, but also because I had let him kiss me the first night we had met and had hardly hesitated when he suggested we should go to Paris together.

I felt sure he would expect me to have made love to heaps of different men, and I wondered if, like David, he would find me unattractive and a bore once he realised how ignorant I was.

I became more and more nervous and frightened, and

while I kept telling myself I had to be brave and remember I was doing this for David, it didn't seem to help.

Finally, I got into the double bed with its pretty pink eiderdown.

There were big vases of carnations in the room and I thought miserably that with only small lights at the bedside, it all looked very seductive.

I was very tense and found it difficult to breathe. So I gripped my fingers together and told myself I must be sensible.

'Perhaps Victor won't realise,' I thought, 'how inexperienced I am.'

He was obviously attracted to me and that should be enough.

I tried to argue myself into the right frame of mind, but I kept thinking of David and how silly I had been not to go away with him to that little inn in the Chilterns.

I felt it would have been so wonderful to let him teach me about love and I would not have been afraid, but only happy with that wild, marvellous ecstasy I felt when he kissed me.

But I told myself severely that even if I had gone with him when he suggested it, he would still have found me boring.

I couldn't help being ignorant about things which no-one had taught me, and perhaps after to-night I should be quite a different person, really sophisticated and poised, like Lady Bettine and all the other women whom David admired.

I was so intent on thinking of David and what he meant to me, that it was quite a shock when I heard the door open and Victor came in.

He was looking exceedingly handsome and attractive in a blue dressing-gown which matched the colour of his eyes.

He closed the door behind him then he stood looking at me with a smile on his lips before he walked towards the bed.

It seemed to me that he walked very, very slowly, and then when he reached my side he said with that beguiling note in his voice which he used when he wanted to be particularly charming:

"That is what I have been waiting for, Samantha."

Then something snapped – I gave a little cry and put my hands up to ward him off.

"I can't! Oh, Victor, I . . . can't! I'm sorry, but I've made a mistake . . . a terrible mistake . . . You'll never forgive me . . . but I shouldn't have come."

My words seemed to fall over themselves, and now the tears were running down my cheeks as I tried frantically, desperately to make him understand.

"I thought . . . I could do it, but I . . . can't!" I cried. "It's wrong . . . and I don't love you and I thought . . . it wouldn't matter to you . . . but now . . . I know it's wicked . . . and I can't . . . please, Victor . . . I can't . . ."

He looked astonished and then he sat down on the side of the bed facing me.

"What is all this about, Samantha?" he asked.

"I oughtn't to have . . . come," I sobbed, "but I thought once I got here everything would be . . . all right . . . and I do like you . . . I do! But now it's come to the point . . . I'm frightened . . . and I knew all the time it was a . . . sin."

My voice was choked for a moment and then Victor said in a surprised tone:

"Are you telling me, Samantha, that no-one has ever made love to you before?"

"No-one," I answered, "and I realise how . . . boring and stupid it makes me . . . but I thought if you . . . taught me about . . . love I would be quite . . . different, and then . . ."

"Then?" Victor prompted.

". . . the man . . . I really love wouldn't find me a . . . bore!" I blurted out.

I thought that might make Victor angry and I put out my hands towards him and said:

"Please don't be ... cross. I'll pay you back every ... penny that you have spent in bringing me here... but after all ... I can't let you ..."

The tears were pouring down my cheeks and I didn't sound very coherent.

Victor took a handkerchief out of the pocket of his dressing-gown and wiped my eyes.

"Don't cry, Samantha," he said gently. "I am trying to understand what all this is about."

"I have been such a ... fool," I told him, "in thinking I could let you ... teach me ... what I ... wanted to know, but Daddy was right when he ... said I must ... keep myself for the man I ... love."

I gave a little sob and added:

"Unfortunately ... the man I love doesn't ... want me."

"Has he said so?" Victor asked.

"He said I was ... absurdly innocent and a ... crashing bore," I answered, and even to say the words made me start to cry all over again.

"Poor Samantha!" Victor said sympathetically.

Then as I put his handkerchief up to my eyes to try to stop the tears he said:

"It's David Durham, isn't it?"

"Y-yes," I answered, "but how ... did you ... ?"

"I heard you had been about with him," Victor answered, "and that he was in love with you. Somebody told me that Durham was caught at last."

I shook my head.

"He likes sophisticated, experienced women," I explained, "and you were quite right when you said I was a fake. I am! I look one way, but I am quite, quite different ... inside."

"I also told you, if you remember," Victor answered,

"that I wanted to know what there was beneath the Bariatinsky model."

"There's nothing!" I said miserably, "except a stupid, idiotic little girl from a Vicarage."

Victor laughed, but not unkindly.

"You are very young, Samantha," he said after a moment.

"I'm getting older," I answered, "but I don't seem to get any more . . . sensible or more experienced."

"I know a lot of men, including myself, who would like you just as you are," Victor said.

He was holding my hand very tightly in his and I thought how kind he was. Then I said in a very small voice:

"Victor . . . will you tell me . . . something?"

"What do you want to know?" he asked.

"What really . . . happens when two . . . people make . . . love?" I asked. "I can't find anything about it in books."

He looked at me in a speculative manner almost as if he questioned what I was saying. Then he answered slowly:

"I think one day, Samantha, someone you love and who loves you will be better qualified to tell you that than I am."

He suddenly got up from the bed and walked across the room to the mantelpiece.

"When I meet David Durham," he said in a strange voice, "I'll knock his damned head off."

"You mustn't do that," I said quickly, "I wouldn't want you to hurt him. It's not his fault that I am so stupid."

Victor didn't answer and after a moment I said nervously:

"Would you like me to go . . . away to-night? I expect I can get a train to Calais and go home by boat . . . or will it do in the morning?"

I spoke in rather a frightened voice because I didn't understand why Victor was angry with David when really he ought to be furious with me.

He turned round and walked back to my side.

"I've decided what we'll do, Samantha," he said. "We'll stay in Paris and enjoy ourselves, you and I, but you must promise me one thing."

"What is that?" I asked nervously.

"That you will try to forget that you are unhappy. I can't bear to see a pretty girl in tears."

"Do you mean I can stay to-morrow?" I asked.

"Just as we planned," he said. "I didn't mean to take you back until the evening because I want to go to the races and I know you will enjoy that too."

"I've cost you a lot of money and ruined your week-end," I said.

"You promised me you wouldn't be miserable," he replied, "and my week-end isn't ruined. I'm determined we'll have fun! So cheer up, Samantha."

"I'm trying to," I answered, "but you are so kind, it makes me want to cry!"

He laughed at that and then he said:

"I'm going to kiss you good-night, Samantha, as I did last night. I like kissing you. Do you like kissing me?"

"I like it very much," I answered.

I thought that was true, and if I had never been kissed by David I would have thought Victor's kisses were rather marvellous.

But he didn't sweep me up to the sky as David did, and there wasn't that strange, wild ecstasy which made me feel as if the whole world had disappeared and there was only David and I alone and part of each other.

Because I was sorry I had behaved so badly I lifted my face up to Victor's and he put his arms round me and kissed me gently and not really passionately, for a long time. Then he said:

"Go to sleep, Samantha, and don't worry about anything. We are going to have a splendid time together to-morrow, and we'll go on seeing each other just as if this had never happened."

"Can we really do that?" I asked.

"You know I never accept defeat," he answered.

I didn't know what he meant by that, but he kissed me again and then he went away shutting the door behind him.

Only when he had gone did I feel I hadn't thanked him enough for being so kind and understanding.

But I told myself I would say it to-morrow.

The next day was an absolute whirl from the moment I got up until we started for home in the evening rather later than we had intended.

We lunched at a very fashionable place overlooking the Seine, and then we went to Longchamps which is the prettiest racecourse I have ever seen.

Once again Victor seemed to know everybody and introduced all sorts of charming Frenchmen who insisted on backing horses for me which always seemed to win.

I came away with quite a wad of francs, although I was not quite certain if I was really entitled to them.

We had tea at Rumplemeyers in the Rue de Rivoli, where they had the most gorgeous cream cakes I have ever tasted in my life. Victor said I was the only person who could afford to eat them because they were guaranteed to put on weight.

Afterwards we went to the Ritz Bar where apparently Victor had asked a lot of people to join us.

We had a kind of cocktail party, only it was more fun and much more amusing than any cocktail party I had ever been to before.

I was really quite sorry when it was time to go home but I knew I had to get back to work on Monday morning and

Victor told me that he had to go North to try out a special racing-car which had been made for him.

It was a lovely clear evening when we set off from Le Bourget and Victor had brought a bottle of champagne because he said we must drink each other's health up in the sky.

It was really rather fun popping the cork as we flew over France and drinking out of small glasses because then we were not so likely to upset the champagne over ourselves.

He had also brought smoked salmon and paté sandwiches to eat and we talked rather more on the way home than we had on the way over.

Even so, it was rather hard to hear and as we drove home from Croydon in Victor's car it seemed very quiet after the noise of the aeroplane engine.

As we got near London I said rather hesitatingly:

"I . . . I want to say . . . thank you, but I don't know how to begin."

"I want to say something to you, Samantha," Victor answered.

"What is that?" I enquired.

"As you know, I have to go North to-morrow, but I expect to be back on Thursday. I want you to think about me while I'm away."

"Of course I shall," I answered, "but why, particularly?"

"Because I have fallen in love with you," he answered, "and when I come back I'm going to do my damndest to make you fall in love with me!"

I looked at him in consternation. That was the last thing I had expected to hear.

His eyes were on the road, his jaw looked very square and then he said quietly:

"I love you, Samantha, and I want to marry you. I don't want you to give me an answer now because I know you are in love with David Durham. But just think about me."

"I will," I promised. "But, oh, Victor, I never expected you to be in love with me."

"I didn't expect it either," he answered, "but you are everything that a man would want in a woman."

"Am I really?" I asked, thinking that the one person who didn't want me was David.

"I didn't mean to settle down so soon," Victor went on, "but now I have met you I am far too frightened of losing you to hang about. The very moment you say you'll marry me, Samantha, I'll sweep you up the aisle so fast that you won't get a chance to change your mind."

"It wouldn't be fair to marry you unless I loved you – really loved you," I said.

"I will make you love me sooner or later," Victor replied. "The only question is – how long will it take?"

As he spoke he drew up outside my flat.

We got out of the car, he carried in my luggage and set it down in the Sitting-room. Then he took me in his arms and kissed me in the same passionate, possessive manner that he had done before we went to Paris.

"I love you!" he said. "Do you promise that you will think about me, Samantha?"

"Of course I will."

Then with his usual abruptness Victor left me and I heard his car drive away.

Reflection 22

I had been thinking of Victor as I spoke and remembering how kind he had been to me, so that I had almost forgotten David was lying beside me and I was really talking to him.

But now I suddenly felt embarrassed that he would think, as he had thought before, that I was trying to blackmail him into marriage by telling him about Victor.

It suddenly swept over me that I had been even more stupid than I had ever been in the past in telling David what had happened and showing him how idiotic I was.

I had made him realise, if he did not know it already, that I was a complete and utter failure when it came to learning about love.

He didn't speak and I felt I knew what he was thinking and how much he despised me.

I had been right in the first place, I told myself, in being determined not to see David again until I was quite sure that I was no longer either ignorant or a bore.

Instead of which I had blurted out how I had upset two kind and charming men and I was still the silly little girl from the Vicarage who had bored and exasperated him.

Why he should ask me to marry him I had no idea, except perhaps he felt a sense of duty because I had been ill.

There was one thing which I knew I must never do, and that was to accept a proposal from David simply because he felt he ought to make it.

I loved him too much to take second best, and if nothing else, what I had been through had taught me that Love can be a two-edged weapon.

Still David didn't speak and at last I said:

"I've only told you this so that you can see how hopelessly incompetent I am. I've tried, David, I've really tried to be what you want. But when it came to the point, I couldn't let Victor make love to me. He was so kind about it . . . and I expect you are laughing at my stupidity . . ."

I gave a sob and went on:

"That is why you must go away. I can't see you any more . . . I couldn't go through all this unhappiness again . . . Perhaps one day I shall manage to improve myself, but it is obviously going to take time."

Again there was silence. Then David said:

"Do you still love me, Samantha?"

"You know I do," I answered. "I've tried to explain that I was doing all this only because I thought it would make me able to please you, but nothing seemed to go . . . right."

I sighed.

"I suppose I'm just made differently from other people, or else it's because of my upbringing. I don't know what it is . . . but I can't help it! I did my very . . . very best and I failed . . . that's all there is to it."

The tears had come into my eyes while I was speaking and now they were running down my cheeks, but I thought David wouldn't realise it because it was dark. I tried to keep my voice steady, but there was a sort of quiver and a break in it.

"I've got a lot to say to you, Samantha," David said at last, "but it's very late and I think you ought to go to sleep."

I would have protested but he went on:

"You've been through a lot this evening. I can understand that seeing me was a shock, and the burglar was an upset which must never happen again. Now that I'm here and no-one can hurt you, I want you to shut your eyes and try to sleep."

He spoke almost coaxingly as if to a child, and then he went on:

"To-morrow I have not only a lot of things to tell you but also something to show you."

"To show me?" I asked.

"In the country," he answered, "and I know you like going to the country."

"What about the Studio?"

"I'll fix that with Bariatinsky," he answered.

"He won't like it if I take a day off," I said. "I was away so long and there is a lot of work for me to do."

"I think he'll understand when I speak to him," David said.

I was rather doubtful, because I know how furious Giles gets if any of us are off work when he has special orders, but I suddenly felt too tired to argue.

I suppose David was right. What with the shock of seeing him and the burglar and the strain of telling him what had happened with Peter and Victor, it was suddenly difficult to keep my eyes open.

"Give me your hand," David said and obediently I put out my hand in the dark.

He took it in his, then he lifted it to his lips.

"Good-night, my darling," he said softly.

I felt a sudden thrill run through me – it was the way David always made me feel which no-one else had ever been able to do.

It was what I had missed with Victor, when he kissed me. It was what no other man could give me!

Instinctively my fingers must have tightened on David's.

He kissed my hand again and then deliberately laid it down in front of me on top of the bed-clothes.

"Go to sleep," he said again.

Surprisingly, although there were so many things I wanted to think about, I obeyed him.

Reflection 23

I woke up thinking I had dreamt of David and then I heard the sound of rushing water.

I thought for a moment that I must be near a river, then I realised that someone was running the bath and I knew it was David.

It was true then what had happened last night! He really had brought me home, and because I had been so frightened after the burglar had struck me, he had stayed the night on my bed!

It seemed impossible! I turned to look and saw the pillow had a dent in it and the eiderdown was thrown back. There was also his dinner-jacket over the chair and his shoes on the floor beside it.

I was trying to remember exactly what he had said and what had happened when he came out of the bathroom.

"You've got the smallest bath I have ever tried to wash in," he said. "For one moment I thought you would have to send for a plumber to gouge me out of it!"

"It's big enough for me," I smiled.

"That's why I'm running your bath," he said slowly. "Hurry, Samantha, we have a long way to go."

He smiled at me.

"You look very pretty in the morning," he said and added:

"While you are getting dressed I'm going to do some telephoning. There are quite a lot of things I have to arrange. And what about breakfast? I see you have some eggs."

"Do you like them scrambled?" I asked.

"I'm not particular," he answered. Then he went into the Sitting-room, closing the door behind him.

I jumped out of bed, had my bath, and started to dress.

While I did so I put the coffee on, and when I was ready in a Chanel-type green suit, which I had managed to buy very cheaply when I first came back to London, I started cooking the eggs.

I remembered that David had a large appetite and fortunately I had bought enough to last me to the end of the week.

I toasted some bread and put butter and marmalade on a tray and carried it into the Sitting-room.

David was just putting down the receiver, and I saw that the chairs were the right way up and he had picked up a number of ornaments which the burglar had thrown off the mantelpiece and from the top of the shelves.

It always seems to me extraordinary that people want to break pretty things. There's something quite horrible and destructive about it, like pulling off butterflies' wings.

Perhaps it's because they feel rebellious or jealous that other people should have things they haven't got themselves.

There was a small gatelegged table in the Sitting-room on which I had my own meals. David opened it for me and I told him where to find a table-cloth and I put down the tray.

I went back to fetch the coffee and we sat down just like an old married couple to eat our breakfast.

The Sitting-room looked untidy but not half as bad as it had seemed last night immediately after the burglar had left.

"Will you bring a few things for the night?" David asked. "I'm going to take you to stay with my cousin."

I looked surprised and he said:

"She is over sixty and will be a very efficient chaperon, I assure you."

His eyes twinkled and I knew he was teasing me, but not in the least unkindly.

"I would like to meet her," I said. "What's her name?"

"It's Kathleen Dunne," he answered. "She has never married and is rather given to 'good works'. You two should get along well together."

"I think you are being unkind to me," I protested.

"Am I?" David asked. "I didn't mean to, Samantha, I want you to be very happy."

There was something in the way in which he said the last words that made my heart give a silly leap.

He got up from the table and said:

"Come on. We must get going. I shall have to stop at my flat on the way because I can hardly arrive in the country wearing a dinner-jacket. I've rung my servant and told him to have everything ready so that I shall not keep you waiting more than a few minutes."

I gathered from this that he didn't intend to ask me to go into the flat and I was glad.

I knew it would have reminded me of the last time I had been there and how we had fought with each other and David had won the battle by completely annihilating me!

I was determined not to think of what had happened after that, or how unhappy I had been.

David had come back again into my life and I tried to tell myself it was wonderful just to be with him, to know he was beside me, and there was no use in thinking too much about the future.

At the same time nothing could prevent my feeling a thrill when he took my arm, when he helped me into the Bentley, and when he looked at me in just his own particular manner which made me feel breathless and excited.

"What is it about being in love," I asked myself, "that makes one feel so totally and completely different from the way one feels with anyone else?"

There was no answer to this question, so I snuggled down in the seat and thought how marvellous it was to be driving beside David again and going with him to the country.

I wondered what his cousin was like and hoped she wouldn't disapprove of me.

Even in my green suit with a plain cloche hat over my red hair I knew I still looked exotic, and not a bit the type of plain, sensible country-girl who I felt would be the sort of young woman David's cousin would think suitable for him.

We arrived at David's flat, and having parked the car outside he said:

"I'll be just as quick as I can, so don't run away until I get back."

"I won't do that," I promised.

He ran up the steps and I wondered whether anyone would think it was strange seeing him return at ten o'clock in the morning still in his dinner-jacket.

Then I thought if anyone did see him they would be quite certain he had spent the night with some charming lady. Perhaps someone like Lady Bettine.

But David had spent the night with me, and I wondered if anyone would ever believe that he had only kissed my hand although we lay side by side in the darkness.

I knew that Melanie and Hortense wouldn't believe it and they would have been frightfully envious of my being alone all night with David Durham, whom they admired enormously.

"Does he really want to marry me?" I asked myself.

That was what he had said, but in a voice which didn't sound quite like him. There was nothing authoritative about it as there had been in the past when he was telling me what I should and should not do.

It was almost as if he were pleading with me, and yet I could not believe that where David was concerned.

Almost before I had time to sort it all out, David came back. He was carrying a suitcase and was dressed in grey flannel trousers with a tweed jacket.

He looked terribly attractive, and though he appeared countrified I knew one thing, that no-one could ever mistake David for anything but a gentleman.

He got into the car, smiled at me and said:

"You are still here. I was rather apprehensive."

"What did Giles say?" I asked. "I had really forgotten about him."

"He grumbled a bit," David answered, "but I think he realises that I have a prior claim where you are concerned."

"Have you?" I asked.

"You know I have," he answered almost fiercely.

I couldn't think of an answer to that so I looked ahead and said nothing.

David put a small flat parcel into my lap.

"A present for you," he said. "I have collected quite a lot of things one way and another that I want to give you, but some of them may have to wait until Christmas."

"Oh, not as long as that!" I exclaimed.

He smiled.

"Open what I have brought you now to start with, at any rate."

I undid the ribbon with which the parcel was tied and opened the tissue paper. Inside was a scarf, one of the fashionable ones which all the most elegant women wore, and I saw it was green and printed with a floral pattern and love-birds.

"Oh, thank you!" I said. "It will exactly match what I am wearing."

"That's what I thought," David said.

I put it round my neck and felt very smart.

I had never been able to afford all the accessories which really make an outfit, however elegant it may be by itself. Giles had provided me with the essentials, but I hadn't fel justified in spending extra money on the scarves, hand-bags and gloves which I had often longed for.

"Thank you," I said again. "Thank you very much! Do you really mean you have some other presents for me?"

"I bought quite a lot of things in New York, the first time I was there," David answered. "I kept seeing things which made me think of you, and as the film was going rather well I thought I might be extravagant."

"I want to hear all about it," I said.

"I'll tell you about it later," David answered. "I'm concerned now with driving very fast so that we shall be there in time for lunch."

I thought that meant we would be lunching with his cousin, and I felt a little disappointed as I had hoped that we would go to an inn where we could talk.

But I knew David had planned the day and I didn't wish to interfere. All I wanted was to relish every moment that we were together.

I realised now just how much I had missed him and how it really had been like losing an arm or a leg because he had not been there.

I knew as we drove along that I could never marry Victor although he is actually better-looking than David. He is also gayer, more amusing, and of course richer; but nothing that Victor could say or do, even though I like him very much, could affect me as one glance or one touch from David did.

I felt as though I was throbbing all over with a kind of inexpressible joy just because he was beside me. Everything seemed full of sunshine and the Bentley was enchanted as it carried us along in a little world of our own where no-one could interrupt us.

We stopped for petrol, and while the tank was being filled up David looked in through the open window on my side and said:

"Are you happy, Samantha?"

Our eyes met and I thought he knew there was no need for me to answer him.

"I am very happy!" I answered in a low voice.

"I can hardly believe you are here," he said, "after . . ."

He didn't finish the sentence as the man said: "It's full, Sir," and he turned away to pay for the petrol.

We drove on again and now we were out of the traffic and moving along country roads. I didn't ask David where we were going. I felt almost absurdly that anywhere would be Paradise as long as he was there.

Vaguely I knew we were somewhere in Oxfordshire. The country-side was very beautiful.

David drove very fast and it must have been a quarter to one o'clock when we turned in at some drive gates and in front of us was an avenue of oak trees.

"Is this where your cousin lives?" I asked.

"No, she lives about two miles away," he said. "This is a house I want you to see and where we are lunching."

As he spoke the drive came to an end and there in front of us was one of the loveliest old houses I had ever seen.

I knew from what Peter had taught me that it was early Elizabethan and might once have been a Priory.

The red bricks had mellowed with age until they seemed almost to glow. The windows were gabled and there were twisting chimney-pots, almost like something out of a fairy-tale, standing high above the roof.

"It's lovely!" I exclaimed.

"I thought you would think so," David answered.

There were smooth green lawns, old yew-hedges and flower-beds which were a riot of gloriously coloured dahlias.

We drove up to the front door and David said:

"Will you wait here a moment, Samantha? I just want to check that everything is arranged for us to see the house."

I wondered who owned it, and I thought anyone who lived in such perfect surroundings was very lucky.

Far in the distance I could see blue hills and all round the house there were trees, some of them very old, which must have stood there for centuries.

David came back smiling.

"It's all right," he said. "Come in. There's a cold lunch waiting for us, but we have to help ourselves. I don't suppose you mind that."

"No, of course not," I answered.

He suggested I might want to wash my hands, and told me to go upstairs.

"There is a door at the top of the landing," he said, "and a bathroom next to it."

The stairs were very old with bannisters of carved oak and newels of strangely fashioned animals at each turn.

The Hall was panelled and on the walls there were portraits -- obviously ancestors – of pretty women and distinguished looking men, most of them in uniform.

The Bed-room was charming, low-ceilinged with a bow-window overlooking a formal garden which contained a sun-dial.

There was a four-poster bed with curtains of blue velvet, and the room smelt of pot-pourri which made me feel homesick because it reminded me of the one Mummy had made from the roses and lavender in our garden.

When I went downstairs David was waiting for me in the Hall.

"I'm going to show you the house after lunch," he said, "but I think we will eat first because I'm hungry."

"I'm afraid the breakfast I gave you wasn't very adequate."

"You did your best, but I am a growing man!"

We laughed at that and then he took me into the Dining-room which was also panelled, and had heavy oak beams running across the ceiling and a medieval fireplace.

There was a long refectory table with two places laid at the end of it and on the sideboard a collection of dishes.

There was cold ham and chicken mayonnaise with a delicious salad to go with it, and for pudding there was apple meringue, which I had not eaten for years.

"I expect the apples are out of the garden," I remarked to David.

"I'm sure they are," David answered. "They didn't know we were coming until I telephoned at breakfast-time, and there certainly wouldn't have been time to go to the shops."

"Why? Is the village far from here?" I asked.

"Nearly two miles," he answered.

"I see you know this place well."

"It belonged to one of my relations," he replied. "That's why I wanted you to see it."

"I think it is one of the most attractive houses I have ever seen," I told him.

There was white wine to drink with our lunch, and a Stilton cheese which David enjoyed more than the apple meringue.

When we had finished he said:

"Now, Samantha, I want to show you the house."

"Was your relative who lived here called Durham?" I asked.

"No," David answered. "The name was Wycombe – Lord Wycombe."

I looked surprised because although everyone was always talking about David, no-one had ever said anything about his social connections. Knowing how 'snobby' some people could be, I thought it strange that no-one had mentioned he was connected with the peerage.

I didn't question David. He was busy taking me back to the Hall where he opened the door of the Drawing-room.

It was a lovely room with white panelled walls and long French-windows opening out into the garden.

The furniture was rather old-fashioned but comfortable, and the chintzes were mellow with age and reminded me of ours at the Vicarage.

The whole house had a very 'lived-in', cosy look, and while I realised that some of the covers were badly faded and occasionally a carpet looked threadbare, it all seemed to blend harmoniously with the age of the house itself.

We walked through the Drawing-room and into the Library which made me exclaim with delight because there were so many books.

There was a Gun-room with a big table in the centre of it and glass-fronted cupboards in which the guns were kept when they were not in use.

We went upstairs and I saw that all the rooms were as charming as the one in which I had tidied myself before lunch. They also had delightful names like 'The Queen Room', because as David explained, it was rumoured that Queen Elizabeth had once stayed there.

There was 'The Duke's Room' and 'The Captain's Room', referring to a Sea-Captain who had commanded a man-o'-war in the first Duke of Marlborough's time.

They all opened off one long passage at the end of which was a baize-covered door. David opened it and I thought we were going into the servants' quarters, but instead there was a Nursery.

It was just like the big Nursery at the Castle before the Butterworths bought it and where Daddy had played as a little boy, and my own Nursery at the Vicarage was similar only on a much smaller scale.

There was a comfortable arm-chair in front of the fire-place which had a brass-rail on which children's clothes could be dried; there was a screen covered with transfers, Christmas cards and scraps which had been varnished over.

There was a toy fort in one corner of the room, a very old one which looked as if it might have belonged to little boys for centuries, and a rocking horse which had lost its tail stood in front of the window.

There was a table in the middle of the room with a heavy blue table-cloth just like the one on which I used to eat my bread and milk.

Through an open door I could see the Night Nursery with a narrow bed for the Nanny and a cot with sides which could let down.

"What a lovely Nursery!" I exclaimed to David.

I walked towards the fort and then I saw a cupboard beside it.

I opened the door and there, as I expected, were the toys: battered building-bricks, a skipping-rope, a top, a box of tin soldiers – and a teddy-bear.

I picked it up and held it in my arms.

"This is just like my teddy-bear, except that mine had lost an eye," I told David. "I used to worry in case he minded being blind."

"Come here, Samantha," David said. "I want to talk to you."

He spoke in such a strange way that I turned round. He was standing in the centre of the room.

"What is it?" I asked.

"Come and sit down," he answered.

There was a small chintz-covered sofa by the window and we sat down on it. Because I still had the teddy-bear in my arms, I set him on my knee.

"You talked to me last night, Samantha," David began, "and now I have a lot of things to say to you."

I felt rather worried because of the serious manner in which he was speaking. But he didn't look at me and after a moment he said:

"I suppose really I should start by apologising. I knew

two minutes after you had run away from me that day in the flat that I had behaved brutally, almost criminally to you."

I made a little sound of protest but he went on:

"I have no excuses for what I said, Samantha, except that perhaps you will understand why I behaved in such a manner when I tell you about myself. It is something I ought to have done long ago."

I didn't answer and he went on:

"I was brought up in this house by my Uncle because my parents died when I was quite young. I loved my Aunt as if she were my mother. She was a sweet and gentle person, but my Uncle was a hard, unbending character.

"He had commanded the Coldstream Guards at one time and spoke to me as if I was a raw recruit in need of discipline.

"While my Aunt was alive, I suppose she protected me from my Uncle, but when she died I found he was impossible to live with.

"I left school and as the War was on I went into the Army when I was seventeen-and-a-half. When I was eighteen I had four months in France, fighting in the trenches, before the War ended. It revolutionised everything I had thought and believed in until then."

David drew in his breath as if he was remembering the horror of it before he went on:

"When the War was over my Uncle wished me to continue in the Regiment or else go to Oxford. But I had no wish to go back to school and I had had enough of soldiering.

"We quarrelled bitterly and because I would not do what he wanted he tried to force me into obeying him. But that was fatal as far as I was concerned: I was already rebellious against the existing order of things because of what I had seen in France.

"I told my Uncle that I would manage to live on my own without his assistance and he could keep what money was mine until I was of age. Then I would come and claim it."

David gave a little laugh.

"I must have sounded very defiant, and I suppose my Uncle thought it would do me good to learn the hard way that I must be dependent on him. He literally cut me off without a shilling!

"Fortunately I had a hundred pounds in the Bank and I set off round the world with a friend. We walked; we hitch-hiked; and we worked our way. I did too many different jobs to even remember them now.

"Some were amusing, some were unspeakably horrible, but I did them because I wouldn't give in. By the time I was twenty I had seen a lot of the world and learnt through a series of mistakes to look after myself quite competently.

"A friend in Singapore suggested I should write an article and send it to a newspaper in England. I took his advice and the newspaper accepted the article with alacrity and paid me far more than I had expected.

"In a year's time I was writing almost continuously for newspapers all over the world. I certainly didn't make a fortune, but I lived a little better than I should have done otherwise.

"I had changed my name because when I left England I didn't want any favours because I was Lord Wycombe's nephew.

"The family name is Dunne, and I changed mine to 'Durham'. I stayed away from England for six years. When I came back I had achieved quite a success in America with the first book I had written.

"It was half a travel book, half an autobiography, with some parts entirely fictional and it was a success. I had now found I could write and knew it was something I enjoyed doing.

"I claimed what was my inheritance and found that my Uncle seemed to have shrunk in stature since I went away. I was no longer afraid of him. I realised he was only a narrow-minded, bigoted old man with whom I would never be likely to have anything in common.

"After a short time in England I went off again abroad. I wrote another travel book, then finally *Vultures Pick Their Bones*."

David took a deep breath.

"As you know, Samantha, it became an overnight success, and of course that meant that I was a success too, and it went to my already swollen head!"

I made a little murmur of protest and he said:

"After you left me and I couldn't find you, I realised just how spoilt and conceited I had become. Because I was continually in the newspapers, because I was spoken of as being a controversial personality, I had begun to think of myself as someone pretty important!"

He paused and went on:

"And of course, Samantha, you will understand when I tell you there were a lot of women.

"There have always been women in my life, but none of them ever meant anything special to me, and I never stayed long enough in one place to find any woman essential to my happiness."

His voice deepened.

"That was – until I met you."

I sat looking at him, holding the teddy-bear as it were protectively in my arms.

"You are so lovely, Samantha, and so different from any woman I had ever met, that I was captivated by you from the first moment I saw you. But I didn't understand."

"What didn't you . . . understand?" I asked.

"That you were the embodiment of all I had wanted, all I had dreamt of and hoped existed somewhere in the world for me as the other part of myself," David answered.

"I suppose," he went on, "you were something too big for

me to grasp, especially as I was eaten up with my own conceit."

He added quickly as I would have spoken:

"No, that is the truth. I had begun to think of myself as irresistible. That was why, Samantha, I couldn't understand that your principles could mean more than the fact that I wanted you.

"Put into words, that sounds ghastly, doesn't it? But it's the truth. Because I knew that you loved me, that you belonged to me in a way no-one else ever had, it gave me a sense of power.

"I imagine all men have a cruel streak in them somewhere. It was that streak, combined with my desire to show my authority over you, that made me continually strike away the radiance I saw in your face with a harsh word.

"Your eyes are very sensitive and very expressive, Samantha. At times I couldn't resist hurting you, simply because your feelings were mirrored so clearly as it made me feel omnipotent. Then you defied me and I couldn't believe it possible that I would not subdue you into doing what I wanted.

"That day when I rang you up and told you I was going to America, my first feeling, even though I was excited about the film, was a frightful sense of loss because I had to leave you.

"But I wouldn't tell you so! I was too busy thinking how clever I was, to humble myself even in love, and God knows I did love you, Samantha."

There was a pain in his voice which made me say:

"Don't be . . . upset . . . David."

"Upset?" he answered. "What do you think I suffered when I couldn't find you? When I thought I had lost you and realised what a fool I had been! Not only a fool, Samantha, but a brute! A man who had no right to your love, because he was utterly and completely despicable!"

"No . . . David . . . no!" I murmured.

"It is true," he said. "I faced myself and found in my shoes an extremely unpleasant person; someone I had not realised existed."

He paused for a moment before he went on:

"Oscar Wilde said, 'Each man kills the thing he loves'. Because I was angry with you, Samantha; because I wanted to hurt you when you wouldn't give in to me; because as it happens, you had unjustly accused me; I wanted to be cruel to you, and I succeeded."

He turned to look at me and said:

"First of all, let me tell you that Bettine Leyton was not travelling with me as my mistress. We had had a love-affair many years before which meant very little to either of us. I had in fact introduced her to my publisher – Frank Leyton – whom she married. When I had the telegram asking me to go to Hollywood, he said they would both go with me."

I gave a little exclamation and David added:

"What you thought was entirely understandable, especially after the way I behaved at Bray Park, but it merely accentuated my anger because you had every right to be upset while I was behaving like a cad."

"No . . . David," I said again.

"It is true," he said almost savagely. "Do you suppose I don't know how totally despicable I was? That, Samantha, was why I hurt you and in the effort hurt not only you but myself.

"You see, my darling," he said, his voice deepening, "the thing I loved about you first was that you were ignorant and I had never known a woman less self-assertive, more gentle, more amenable, more divinely humble about her own beauty.

"I loved you for that and there was so much I wanted to teach you. But more than anything else, I loved you because you were innocent. It took me some time to realise how completely unspoilt and pure you were. When I knew it,

185

instead of trying to despoil you, I should have gone down on my knees and thanked God that I had found you before any other man did."

I looked at David in surprise.

"You mean ... you don't mind that I am so ... inexperienced?"

"Do you suppose I want you any other way?" he asked fiercely. "I love you, Samantha. I will kill any other man who touches you. You are mine! Mine, as you have been since the first moment we kissed each other on the Embankment. That wonderful, magical kiss, which I can never forget!"

He made a sound that was almost one of pain, and then he put his arm round me and drew me close to him.

"How can I ever tell you what it means to know that through my criminal stupidity you might have belonged to someone else? I could murder Victor Fitzroy for taking you away with him, if I weren't so overwhelmingly grateful to him for bringing you back still untouched – still *my* Samantha, as you were always meant to be."

"But you may ... still find me a ... bore," I whispered.

My voice was unsteady because thrills were running through me as David's arms were round me and his lips were so near to mine.

"I am in love, Samantha," David answered, "in love as I never imagined it possible to be. They tell me that no-one has ever been bored when in love. You fascinate me, my darling, everything about you is utterly perfect, unique, and unlike any other woman."

"Oh ... David!" I murmured.

"I don't deserve you. If you had any sense you would send me away. But instead will you forgive me and say that you will marry me?"

There was a return of the masterful note in his voice which I knew so well as he went on:

"You see, darling, I can't live without you and I certainly couldn't live here in this big house by myself."

"Here?" I questioned.

"My Uncle is dead," David answered. "I have inherited the Estate. I am also, as it happens, the new Lord Wycombe!"

I gave a little gasp and he went on:

"Do you think you would find it boring, Samantha, two miles from the nearest village? I am not going to let you live in London – you are too beautiful! I also have quite a number of books I want to write. Some will be filmed. Hollywood has already taken an option on them and if we go there we go together. Otherwise I intend to stay here. But I would be very lonely and very unhappy without you, my precious!"

He looked down into my eyes and they must have been shining with the excitement of what he was saying to me.

Then suddenly as if something broke inside him he pulled me closer to him and his lips were on mine.

He kissed me wildly, passionately, frantically and it was even more wonderful and more glorious than it had ever been before.

I had never believed that anyone could feel such perfectly marvellous sensations and not die of happiness.

David raised his head.

"I adore you!" he said. "My sweet, perfect, innocent little love."

Then he was kissing my eyes, my ears, my nose, my chin, and the little pulse that was beating in my neck because I was so excited.

His kisses made me thrill even more than ever, and then his lips were on mine again.

I felt as though he flew me up to the sun and we were both blinded by the wonder of it.

Finally, in a voice I hardly recognised, David said:

"Are you going to marry me? Please say yes, Samantha."

I put my arms round his neck and drew his lips nearer to mine.

"I will . . . marry you on one . . . condition."

"And what is that?" David asked.

"That you will tell me how to . . . fill this wonderful . . . Nursery with lots and lots of . . . our babies," I whispered.

He held me so tightly that it was impossible for me to breathe and then he said unsteadily:

"The answer is – yes, Samantha!"

Other Books by Barbara Cartland

Romantic Novels, over 100,
the most recently published being:

The Shadow of Sin
The Tears of Love
The Devil in Love
Love is Innocent
An Arrow to the Heart
The Elusive Earl

Autobiographical and Biographical

The Isthmus Years 1919–1939
The Years of Opportunity 1939–1945
I Search for Rainbows 1945–1966
We Danced All Night 1919–1929
Ronald Cartland
(with a foreword by Sir Winston Churchill)
Polly, My Wonderful Mother

Historical

Bewitching Women
The Outrageous Queen
(The Story of Queen Christina of Sweden)
The Scandalous Life of King Carol
The Private Life of King Charles II
The Private Life of Elizabeth, Empress of Russia
Josephine, Empress of France
Diane de Poitiers
Metternich – the Passionate Diplomat

Sociology

You in the Home
The Fascinating Forties
Marriage for Moderns
Be Vivid, Be Vital
Love, Life and Sex
Vitamins for Vitality
Husbands and Wives

Etiquette
The Many Facets of Love
Sex and the Teenager
The Book of Charm
Living Together
The Youth Secret
The Magic of Honey
Barbara Cartland's Book of Beauty and Health
Men are Wonderful

Cookery

Barbara Cartland's Health Food Cookery Book
Food for Love
The Magic of Honey Cookery Book

Editor of

The Common Problems by Ronald Cartland
(with a preface by the Rt. Hon. The Earl of Selbourne, P.C.)

Drama

Blood Money
French Dressing

Philosophy

Touch the Stars

Radio Operetta

The Rose and the Violet (Music by Mark Lubbock).
Performed in 1942

Radio Plays

The Caged Bird: An episode in the Life of Elizabeth,
Empress of Austria. Performed in 1957

Verse

Lines on Life and Love

Georgette Heyer
Sprig Muslin 70p

'Amanda Smith, I regret to be obliged to inform you that you
are a shockingly untruthful girl,' said Sir Gareth calmly.

Amanda looked far too young and too pretty in her gown of
sprig muslin to be going about the Regency countryside
unattended – it clearly behoved any man of honour, such as
that noted Corinthian Sir Gareth Ludlow, to restore her to
her family . . .

Unfortunately, Amanda's determination and lively
imagination made this a task fraught with difficulty, and
involved some of the nicest people in quite reprehensible
situations . . .

'The author manages her period conversations with skill
and consistency, and her book, at its various levels, is
exciting and entertaining. Altogether, it is probably the
best thing Miss Heyer has yet done in this kind' PUNCH

Regency Buck 60p

Rich and lovely, ardent and wilful, any restraint maddened
Judith Taverner. But in her handsome guardian she met her
match – and more.

Julian St John Audley, Fifth Earl of Worth, was one of the
Bow-window set, a gamester, an excellent whip and a friend
of Beau Brummell. Merely thinking of him was enough to
put Judith into a rage. Before long she discovered there
were other people who also hated her legal guardian . . .

'From the fashionable world of London to the fashionable
world of Brighton, Miss Heyer draws the background with
an attention to accuracy which is admirable'
THE TIMES LITERARY SUPPLEMENT

Selected bestsellers

- ☐ **Jaws** Peter Benchley 70p
- ☐ **Let Sleeping Vets Lie** James Herriot 60p
- ☐ **If Only They Could Talk** James Herriot 60p
- ☐ **It Shouldn't Happen to a Vet** James Herriot 60p
- ☐ **Vet in Harness** James Herriot 60p
- ☐ **Tinker Tailor Soldier Spy** John le Carré 60p
- ☐ **Alive: The Story of the Andes Survivors** (illus)
  Piers Paul Read 75p
- ☐ **Gone with the Wind** Margaret Mitchell £1.50
- ☐ **Mandingo** Kyle Onstott 75p
- ☐ **Shout at the Devil** Wilbur Smith 70p
- ☐ **Cashelmara** Susan Howatch £1.25
- ☐ **Hotel** Arthur Hailey 80p
- ☐ **The Tower** Richard Martin Stern 70p
  (filmed as *The Towering Inferno*)
- ☐ **Bonecrack** Dick Francis 60p
- ☐ **Jonathan Livingston Seagull** Richard Bach 80p
- ☐ **The Fifth Estate** Robin Moore 75p
- ☐ **Royal Flash** George MacDonald Fraser 60p
- ☐ **The Nonesuch** Georgette Heyer 60p
- ☐ **Murder Most Royal** Jean Plaidy 80p
- ☐ **The Grapes of Wrath** John Steinbeck 95p

All these books are available at your bookshop or newsagent;
or can be obtained direct from the publisher
Just tick the titles you want and fill in the form below
Prices quoted are applicable in UK

Pan Books, Cavaye Place, London SW10 9PG
Send purchase price plus 15p for the first book and 5p for each
additional book, to allow for postage and packing

Name (block letters)————————————————————

Address————————————————————————

————————————————————————————

While every effort is made to keep prices low, it is sometimes
necessary to increase prices at short notice. Pan Books reserve the
right to show on covers new retail prices which may differ from
those advertised in the text or elsewhere